# COMMENTS ON
## HOLMES ADV... FROM
## HUGH ASHTON

"...good pastiches of the Sherlock stories are hard to come by.
I think Mr. Ashton does an extraordinary job of making me feel
like this could have been part of the original Canon."

"For those who love Sherlock Holmes, you will love these
pastiches by Hugh Ashton. Engaging and written in Conan
Doyle's style."

"'The game is afoot' lives on in the writings of Hugh Ashton. If
Sherlock Holmes has intrigued you in the past, gather together
around the dispatch box of John H. Watson series. Get them all
and dig into a welcome return to Sherlock and his cases."

"The last products of the Dispatch Box once owned by John
Watson, M.D. are superbly crafted, including two stories that
Dr. Watson transcribed from Holmes' notes and turned into a
story of some worth."

"There is a consistency of voice and the stories ring true to
the originals. Ashton has become one of the best writers of
Sherlock Holmes stories, and if you are a fan, this is a must."

"When trying to emulate Doyle,
Hugh Ashton is at the top of the list."

# 1894

1894 – Some Adventures of Mr. Sherlock Holmes
Hugh Ashton

ISBN-13: 978-1-912605-04-0
ISBN-10: 1-912605-04-X
Published by j-views Publishing, 2018

This is a work of fiction. Names, characters, places, brands, media, and incidents are either the product of the author's imagination or are written in respectful tribute to the creator of the principal characters.

www.j-views.biz

www.221BeanBakerStreet.info

j-views Publishing, 26 Lombard Street, Lichfield, UK, WS13 6DR

# Contents

## Acknowledgements

Never imagine that a book is the product of one person's hard work. This volume owes much to many people, all over the world.

To all those who know and love the adventures of Sherlock Holmes, and have thereby encouraged me by telling me how they have enjoyed my stories.

To the memory of Jo at Inknbeans Press, whose encouragement and support helped me return time and again to climb the seventeen steps to 221B Baker-street.

And to Yoshiko, who watches patiently as her husband creates and solves murders, thefts and other nefarious crimes.

# Colophon

E decided that this adventure of Sherlock Holmes deserved to be reproduced in paper form in as authentic a fashion as was possible given modern desktop publishing and print-on-demand technology.

Accordingly, after consulting the reproductions of the original Holmes adventures as printed in *The Strand Magazine*, we decided to use the TT Barrels font as the body (10.5 on 13.2). Though it would probably look better letterpressed than printed using a lithographic or laser method, and is missing old-style numerals, it still manages to convey the feel of the original.

The flowers are from the Bodini Ornaments font, which have a little more of a 19th-century appearance than some of the alternatives.

Page headers are in Baskerville (what else can one use for a Holmes story?), and the titles are set in Amarante. The decorative drop caps are in Romantique, which preserves the feel of the *Strand's* original drop caps.

We have tried to carry out the punctuation according to the rules apparently followed by the *Strand*'s typesetters and others from the same period. These include double spacing after full stops (periods), spaces after opening quotation marks, and spaces on either side of punctuation such as question marks, exclamation marks and semi-colons. This seems to allow the type to breathe more easily, especially in long spoken and quoted exchanges, and we have therefore adopted this style here.

Some of the orthography has also been deliberately changed to match the original – for instance, "Baker Street" has become " Baker-street" throughout.

# 1894

## Some Adventures of Mr. Sherlock Holmes

Discovered by

## Hugh Ashton

J-views Publishing, Lichfield, England

# EDITOR'S NOTES

"When I look at the three massive manuscript volumes which contain our work for the year 1894 I confess that it is very difficult for me, out of such a wealth of material, to select the cases which are most interesting in themselves and at the same time most conducive to a display of those peculiar powers for which my friend was famous. As I turn over the pages I see my notes upon the repulsive story of the red leech and the terrible death of Crosby the banker. Here also I find an account of the Addleton tragedy and the singular contents of the ancient British barrow. The famous Smith-Mortimer succession case comes also within this period, and so does the tracking and arrest of Huret, the Boulevard assassin."

John H. Watson M.D. (The Adventure of the Golden Pince-Nez)

HOUGH THICK in terms of the number of pages, this memorandum book of Watson's could not be described as "massive", and it is to be feared that his memory failed him somewhat in this respect when he came to pen the adventure of Willoughby Smith and his untimely death.

However, the accounts in this book all correspond to those mentioned in the published tale. There has been some debate, based on Watson's lack of punctuation, and the use of the "Oxford comma", as to whether the leech and Crosby are the same adventure, or two separate cases. They are, as I discovered, one and the same case.

Likewise, the Addleton tragedy and the barrow – one or two cases? I discovered that here, there were two separate cases involved.

In addition to these cases, there is one more, that of the two Coptic patriarchs, which is written in a slightly different hand, though still unmistakably that of Watson, and using a different pen and ink from the other adventures. We must therefore conclude that Watson used blank pages in the book to pen this tale at a later date. However, I have included it in this collection, since it was located between the same covers as the others.

Here, then, are some of Holmes' adventures in 1894, the year in which most biographers agree he returned to London from his apparent death, to defeat Colonel Sebastian Moran, and to once again confound the wiles of the criminals and evil-doers of the realm.

THE ADVENTURE OF THE RED LEECH: Though Lestrade brings the case to Holmes' attention, he plays a relatively small part in the unmasking of the villain. Watson's skills as a physician are evident here, though with his usual modesty he fails to draw attention to them.

The Adventure of the Addleton Tragedy: Though not a tragedy in the usual sense of the word, both Holmes and Watson describe the events set down here as a tragedy, though each man ascribes a different meaning here.

The Adventure of the Ancient British Barrow: Holmes and Watson leave London to explore the past. This adventure is set in the East Anglian countryside. Holmes' deductive skills and his scientific expertise are shown here, as is his interest in history and archeology.

The Adventure of the Smith-Mortimer Succession: Holmes as a gambler is an unusual depiction of the great detective, but the result of Holmes' efforts in this case rests on a throw of the dice.

The Adventure of the Boulevard Assassin: More of a police adventure than a criminal investigation, Holmes and Watson act as special constables assisting Inspector Stanley Hopkins in his pursuit of an international terrorist.

The Adventure of the Two Coptic Patriarchs: Mentioned in the Adventure of the Retired Colourman, Holmes uncovers a most ingenious attempt at a crime.

In my opinion, these cases are as interesting as those that were published by Watson through Sir Arthur, and it must have been fear of exposure of the principals that prevented them from being published in Watson's lifetime. In the case of Addleton, it is an interesting irony that Holmes demolishes the idea of Spiritualism, given Sir Arthur Conan Doyle's later espousal of it.

*Hugh Ashton*
*Kamakura and Lichfield*
*January 2016*

# THE ADVENTURE OF THE RED LEECH

F ALL THE CASES with which I assisted my friend Sherlock Holmes, none was more repulsive in its minutiae than the affair of Crosby the banker, and his death, the full details of which were never made public.

It began on a November afternoon. Dusk was falling, and the thick fog that wrapped itself around London made the room so dark that we were forced to light the gas before three o'clock. I had dropped in earlier to visit Holmes at the rooms in Baker-street, and found myself trapped by the darkness and fog. No cabs were on the streets, and I had no wish to navigate London in the dark mists that made it impossible to determine one's location. Happily my old bedroom was still available, and I was prepared to spend the night there, and resume my journey home the next day.

I was engaged in a study of the day's newspapers, and Holmes was sawing away idly on his violin, producing tones which, to my ear, were discordant, but appeared to find favour with him.

"It is strange," he remarked, in the intervals of his fiddling, "that the criminal classes do not make use of the fog as much as one would imagine. Were I that way inclined, I would use the cover provided by the inclement weather to work my wicked way upon the good citizens of this great city."

"Then it is lucky for them that you are not of that nature," I replied, laughing.

"Do you know, I was tempted at one time to make my living that way," he told me, with an air of great seriousness. "I realised early on that I had gifts that are denied to the majority, and that those gifts could be used for good or ill."

I had never heard him talk in this way before, and I was curious. "What prevented you from taking the low road of crime? The fear of capture and punishment?"

"By no means. You have seen the average police agent in action, have you not? Can you seriously bring yourself to believe that any of them would have any chance at all of capturing me? Why, even at that early stage of my career, I could plan crimes which were so subtle and ingenious that they might not even be recognised as crimes. What turned me from a potential life of crime? you ask me. That is a speculative question of metaphysics, a branch of enquiry which does not attract me. I cannot say that I have an answer to your question, other than that the challenge of unlocking puzzles is more pleasurable to me than that of setting puzzles for others to unlock." He smiled.

I pondered this, forbearing from further comment, and Holmes resumed his scrapings upon the fiddle. He stopped abruptly in mid-phrase.

"What is that?" he asked. "A client, on a day like this?" His keen hearing had detected a sound that my dull senses had overlooked.

There was a knock on the door, and Inspector Lestrade entered in answer to Holmes' invitation.

"By Jove, it is cold out there," he said. Droplets of moisture clung to his overcoat, and to his muffler wound around his face.

"Come, remove your outer garments and warm yourself by the fire," Holmes urged him, laying down his violin. "Mrs. Hudson will dry them for you."

"And as a medical man, I strongly recommend a good stiff dose of brandy and soda," I told him. In truth, Lestrade appeared unwell, though whether this was the result of the inclement weather, or from another cause, I was unable to tell.

"Thank you," Lestrade said, gratefully accepting the glass I held out to him. "I am glad to see you here today, Doctor. It is a case that may need your expertise, as well as that of Mr. Holmes here."

"You have a case, then?" said Sherlock Holmes, his attention now fixed on Lestrade.

"We do indeed, Mr. Holmes, and nothing other than a case which appears of no solution would induce me to stir outside on an evening such as this. You have been good enough to provide us with one or two hints in the past, Mr. Holmes, and we would very much appreciate your assistance in this matter, as well as your opinions, Doctor."

"The case concerns a senior partner in the banking firm of Lightfoot and Co., of Charing-cross."

"I am familiar with the name," replied Holmes.

"Sir Earnest Crosby is a well-respected member of the banking world, and received his knighthood recently. His wife, Lady Margaret, was a well-known society beauty in the days when she was known as Margaret Locke. They reside, with their three children, in Wimbledon." He took a pull at his drink before proceeding. "The household also contains Lady Margaret's younger brother, Thomas, and Sir Earnest's elderly mother, in addition to the usual domestic staff."

"I seem to recall the name of Thomas Locke in connection with some scandal related to gaming," mused Holmes.

"Indeed so. He was named as one of the parties in a conspiracy to defraud bookmakers at an Epsom race meeting some three years back. Though I personally believe that there was a conspiracy, and that Locke formed a part of it, albeit a small part, the case was thrown out for lack of firm evidence."

"I recall it now," said Holmes. "The case hinged on the similarity of the handwriting on a betting slip with that of one of the accused, and the officer in charge made a sad bungle of the affair, did he not?"

"I would reluctantly accept your opinion of the police in that case," admitted Lestrade. "However, the case on which I am involved appears to be a little more perplexing. Sir Earnest has enjoyed robust health all his life, and it has been a source of pride to him that he has never missed a day at the office in all his years with Lightfoot & Co. Two months ago, however, he rose, prepared himself for the day, and fell to the ground while shaving himself. Although he was not hurt in the fall, he complained of weakness and dizziness."

"This does not sound like a case for the police," I said. "Surely one for a doctor?"

"Naturally, this seemed to be the case," said Lestrade. "Lady Margaret immediately sent for the family physician, who proceeded to examine Sir Earnest, but was unable to discover any immediate cause of this sudden weakness. One singular point presented itself, though. On the pillow of the bed where Sir Earnest had spent the night, there was a small circular bloodstain, and though the doctor examined the patient thoroughly, there was no obvious source from which the blood might have been emitted."

"These country doctors are sometimes less than thorough in their methods," I said. "I do not claim that I would be any more discerning, but I am sure that a Harley-street specialist would be able to make an accurate diagnosis in a very short space of time."

Lestrade smiled at me. "In the case of the Crosby household, the family physician is Sir James Mackenzie, a name with which you may be familiar."

"Indeed so. One of the foremost names in the land in the field of general medicine. I withdraw my comments regarding country physicians."

"I have warned you before," Sherlock Holmes told me, with a not unfriendly smile, "of the danger of forming opinions before all the facts are in."

"Be that as it may," Lestrade continued, "Sir James was of the opinion that the trouble might be nervous or cerebral, and the same day referred his patient to a specialist in these matters. However, the specialist likewise failed to determine any definite cause. A few days' rest saw Sir Earnest seemingly restored to health, and he returned to his work as usual. However, very much the same thing occurred within a week. Sir Earnest collapsed while dressing, and once more, the bloodstain, with no obvious source of the blood, was discovered on the pillow."

"There were no bloodstains to be discovered in the time that Sir Earnest was attending to his duties at the bank?" asked Holmes.

"That is correct. The bloodstains only appeared on the days when Sir Earnest was taken with these fits of weakness in the morning."

"And there have been other incidents, I take it?"

"Several, at intervals of approximately one week. As I mentioned, the first occurred some two months ago, and he has been seized with these symptoms some six times in all since then. In every case, bloodstains have been discovered on the pillow on those mornings, and only on those mornings."

"And how do the police come to be involved with this?"

"The local Chief Inspector is a friend of the family. Lady Margaret enlisted his support following the third incident, and the case was referred to us about one week ago. However, it was felt that there was little we could do in the case, and accordingly little progress has been made. Indeed, I must confess that there has been no progress or action taken by us."

"And you have come to us," said Holmes, "on such an evening as this. I take it there is some urgency?"

"We received a telegram from Chief Inspector Hollander not two hours ago, informing us that Sir Earnest had been taken ill this morning, and his condition, unlike on previous occasions, was critical. I therefore judged it best to enlist your assistance on this case, since the circumstances are such that our usual lines of enquiry might well prove fruitless. Your methods, Mr. Holmes, though unorthodox, have nonetheless proved to be useful on occasion. Doctor Watson's opinions would likewise seem to be of value to us here."

"It is a case that would seem to provide a certain amount of interest. When do we start?"

"You propose visiting the house? Now?"

"Naturally," said Holmes. "You have been informed that Sir Earnest is in critical condition. What better time to investigate the case? The District Railway will take us there, I am sure, even in this foul weather."

"I will bring my medical supplies," I announced. The prospect of action of this kind was welcome to me.

Holmes rang for Mrs. Hudson, and requested her to bring Lestrade's coat and hat.

"I hope you'll dress up warm, gentlemen," she told us, handing over the requested garments. "It's not a night to be out. Do take care of yourself, sir," she addressed Sherlock. "And you, Doctor, and you, sir."

"She concerns herself too much about me," Sherlock Holmes half-grumbled as we made our way to the Baker-street Underground station.

On arrival at Wimbledon, although it was by now dark, the thick fog that had enveloped central London had thinned to a mist, and it was an easy walk to The Yews, the house occupied by Crosby and his family.

On arrival at the large modern red-brick house, close to the Common, the door was opened to us by a young smartly dressed maid, who took our cards, and ushered us into a drawing-room.

Lady Margaret entered a few minutes later. It was clear that in her day she had been a great beauty. She was still a very handsome woman, but her face was marked by lines of worry, and her expression was one of sadness.

"It is good of you to come here, Inspector," she said to Lestrade, "especially on a night such as this. And you, Mr. Holmes and Dr. Watson. I am most grateful to you for your concern."

"How is he?" asked Holmes.

She shook her head sadly. "He is still very weak, and unable to rise from his bed. Sir James Mackenzie is with him now."

"Perhaps I might be permitted to see him?" I ventured. "It may be that my understanding of the symptoms will be of assistance to Holmes when he makes his investigation."

"By all means. You may find, however," she added with a wry smile, "that Sir James has a way with outsiders that is not altogether welcoming."

"I can understand his feelings in the matter. I wish only to observe," I answered.

"Sarah will show you the way," she told me, ringing the bell and directing the maid who had admitted us to escort me to Sir Earnest's room.

The room itself was a large, airy chamber. Sir Earnest was lying there, his eyes closed, and a face as pale as any I had ever seen on any living man. Sir James Mackenzie, whom I recognised from public lectures that I had attended, was standing by the bedside. I introduced myself, and we shook hands.

"I have no intention of interfering with your patient or your treatment of him," I explained. "I am here with Sherlock Holmes, of whom you may have heard, and wish to ascertain the medical facts of the case."

"Before your friend begins to treat this as a criminal matter, eh?" he asked. "Well, I see no harm in that. What have you heard so far?"

I repeated to him the facts as they had been told to us by Lestrade, and he nodded in confirmation. "Yes, that is so, as far as it goes," he said when I had finished.

"There is more?"

"You can see for yourself how pale the patient is. He would have appeared to have lost a significant quantity of blood. The bloodstains on the pillow would seem to point to the same conclusion."

"How big were these stains?"

He shook his head. "Their size hardly correlates with the amount of blood I estimate to have been lost. The largest such was the size of a florin, and the smallest that of a three-penny piece. Each was circular, and the pillowcase alone was stained heavily – the blood had not penetrated to the pillow itself in any significant quantity."

"You would conclude, then, that the blood had been extracted by persons unknown, and stored in some container before its removal from the room?"

He stared at me. "I can tell that your association with Sherlock Holmes has led you to make fanciful conclusions at a moment's notice."

"I am sorry—" I began, but he held up a hand.

"No, no. I meant no criticism. You have reached the same conclusion as have I, except that it took me as many weeks as it has taken you minutes."

"And you have not been able to detect any mark on the patient that would account for such a loss of blood?"

"There would be nothing visible, would there, were a hypodermic needle to be used?"

I was flattered that the famous physician appeared to be treating me as an equal in the discussion. "It would certainly meet the facts of the case," I said. "However, it would seem to require a certain amount of medical skill to accomplish. It is not a procedure I would care to undertake lightly."

"Nor I," he agreed. "However, if I may be permitted to tread in the ground of your friend Holmes, it may be of some significance to note that Lady Margaret's brother, Thomas, studied medicine at Guy's for two or three years before deciding that the profession was not, after all, for him."

"That is a fact well worth knowing," I said. "How did you discover that, if I may ask?"

"He was a student of mine. Not the worst of the class by any manner of means. He certainly possessed a certain skill at dissection in the anatomy classes."

"And what is your prognosis for the patient?" I asked, indicating the recumbent form of Sir Earnest, whose eyes were still closed.

"Not good, I am afraid," Sir James informed me. "Listen to his heart for yourself." He passed his stethoscope to me, and I adjusted it and listened.

"The heartbeat is disturbingly irregular, is it not?" I asked "And weak into the bargain."

He nodded. "That is not consistent with the apparent loss of blood, but is due to some other factor, I believe. The breathing is irregular and laboured, but that is a consequence of the problems with the heart, I think we may safely assume."

"So we must take it that there is an assailant, as yet

unknown, who is removing blood from Sir Earnest, at the same time as administering some drug that is affecting his heart?"

"Indeed. A potentially fatal combination. Especially on this occasion, when the blood loss seems to be greater than before, and the dosage of the drug also greater. I believe in this case, though I have not informed Lady Margaret of this, and I beg you also to keep it a secret from her, that Sir Earnest will not live to see tomorrow's dawn."

"You will be here all night?"

"Or until the end, whichever comes the soonest. I know that we of the medical profession are not expected to display an emotional side, but Sir Earnest and I were firm friends, and it is sad for me to see him in this pitiable state."

"Should you desire some relief in your vigil...?" I suggested.

Sir James shook his head. "No, but I thank you for the generous thought. This is one I must bear alone."

I left him, and rejoined the others in the drawing-room.

"How is he?" Lady Margaret asked me anxiously.

"I cannot say with the authority of Sir James, but I am sorry to say that I fear he is far from well."

"You will not give me a prediction?" There was fear and sadness in her face as she looked into my eyes.

I found it hard to meet her gaze, and looked away. "It is not for me to do that, Lady Margaret. You must ask Sir James for that."

"I fear for my beloved Earnest. Excuse me, gentlemen." She held a handkerchief before her face and rose. "I must see him now, and talk with Sir James. No, do not stir," she requested us.

"Have you learned anything interesting?" Holmes asked, when the door had closed behind our hostess, and we had heard the sound of her footsteps ascending the stairs.

I repeated the gist of my conversation with Sir James.

Lestrade let out a low whistle. "Then it's the brother. I do not know if you remember the Epsom case in detail, but there is a connection."

"By George, yes," said Holmes quietly. "The ring of conspirators was accused of conspiring to inject the favourites with a solution of opium. The man who was appointed to carry out the deed was Thomas Locke."

"The case against him begins to look very clear, then," I said.

"There is definitely evidence that seems to point in his direction," Holmes agreed.

Lestrade yawned. "Gentlemen, I believe that I must leave you at this point. A telegram to the Yard will fetch me should you discover anything that needs my attention. Make my apologies to our charming hostess, if you would." So saying, he left us, and we heard the front door opening and closing as he quitted the house.

"Well!" I said to Holmes. "What do you make of Lestrade's behaviour? Walking out on a case like that?"

Holmes laughed. "He is doing the right thing for once in his life," he said. "Rather than charging at the problem like a bull at a gate, and making an arrest that could be a cause of subsequent embarrassment, he has decided to let me gather further data with which he knows I will present him later, and he will then be enabled to present himself as the detective who solved the Crosby murder."

"And us?"

"Your plans were to spend the night at Baker-street, were they not? I suggest you amend them to a sojourn here in Wimbledon."

"Very well."

Our hostess returned at this point, a sombre look on her face. "He is not at all well, Sir James tells me. He will not say, but I fear he suspects that my poor husband will not survive the night." She appeared ready to sob, but controlled herself with a visible effort. "Do you suspect foul play, Mr. Holmes?"

"I cannot make a pronouncement at this stage," he told her.

"And you, Doctor Watson?" she appealed to me.

"For myself, I am sorry to say that I can see little other alternative," I told her. She looked crest-fallen at this news.

"Where is the police inspector?" she asked, as if noticing his absence for the first time.

"He left for London, Lady Margaret," Holmes replied. "He told us that he wished to consult some documents there that might have a bearing on the case."

Lady Margaret's eyes flashed fire. "If he was referring to the case in which my poor brother was involved a few years back, he is wasting his time," she said, in a passionate tone. "Thomas was young and foolish, and maybe some would still judge him as such, but he would never hurt anyone, least of all Earnest. My husband, you should know, retained the finest legal counsel in the case, and assisted Thomas on his release by providing him with a place in the bank. Thomas owes so much to Earnest. He would never do anything to harm him. Never!"

"No-one has accused your brother of anything, Lady Margaret," Holmes gently reminded her. "Least of all, of injuring your husband."

"But they will, I know it," she said to us, distraught. Her face cleared, and her voice changed. "May we expect the pleasure of your company at dinner tonight? Under the circumstances, I think you may dispense with dressing for dinner. My mother-in-law and my brother will be dining with us, as well as Sir James, if Earnest's condition permits."

"We would be honoured to accept," said Holmes. "Many thanks."

"And you will lodge here tonight?"

"If you permit it," said Holmes, "we will stay here, even if we do not actually go to bed."

"You anticipate some sort of trouble tonight? Some new developments?"

"Not at all, but we have arrived late on the scene of this mystery, and I am keen to make up for lost time. I propose working through the night."

"I see. How original." She smiled faintly. "Now, if you will excuse me, I must prepare myself for dinner."

"The lady doth protest too much," I said to Holmes when we were alone together once more. "No-one even mentioned her brother, and she was quick to defend him as soon as we mentioned that Lestrade had returned to the Yard."

"It does seem as though she is over-jealous of the family honour."

"You think it to be no more than that?"

Holmes shrugged. "Who can say? It is as likely as any other reason, do you not think? In any event, it seems we will meet the brother soon, and be able to form some sort of opinion for ourselves."

Dinner was served with Sir James absent. The physician had expressed his resolve to remain with the patient, and his meal was sent up on a tray. Thomas, the brother, met the impression I had formed of him from his history and reputation. He was, I estimated, some ten years younger than his sister, and though he was dressed immaculately, there was something of the young "swell" about him. He appeared fascinated by my friend, and continually asked him questions about some of the cases in which Holmes had been involved, to which Holmes generally provided courteous and non-committal answers.

By contrast, Mrs. Elvira Crosby, Sir Earnest's mother, sat silently and morosely throughout the meal. The only words that I heard her address were to the servants, demanding that food or drink be served to her. The servants, when addressing her, spoke in loud tones, and I gathered that she was somewhat deaf. Before the meal, Lady Margaret gave thanks, and I noticed her mother-in-law making the sign of the Cross. Given her name, her general appearance, and this last-mentioned action, I judged her to be of Hispanic descent.

After the meal, the ladies withdrew, and Thomas Locke was left with Holmes and myself.

"You are here, I take it, to discover the truth of poor

Earnest's condition?" he asked. "I did not want to raise the subject in front of Margaret, my sister, for I know how devoted she is to him."

"That is why we are here," Holmes confirmed.

"And may I be of assistance?" he asked, eagerly.

I was about to deny him his request, indignant that a man who had been accused of such a crime as had he should even consider that he might be considered as a helper in this matter, but Holmes forestalled me.

"We would be more than grateful, Mr. Locke, if you could answer a few questions to the best of your ability, as frankly as possible. Some of these questions may seem to you to invade on your family's private feelings, but it is important to me to ascertain the facts, just as much as it is Watson's task to ask questions that may seem impertinent in the cause of diagnosing a sickness."

"I understand, and I will do my best."

"Very well, then. You say that your sister is devoted to your brother-in-law. In your opinion, is that devotion returned?"

Locke twisted uncomfortably in his chair. "Your first question is uncomfortably near the mark. I have to say that her devotion is not returned. Earnest is a good man, and he has been of great assistance to me in my troubles, of which you have no doubt heard, but I have to say that my sister's devotion is not fully returned. Please do not ask me to expound further on this matter, I beg you."

"I see. What of your mother-in-law?"

"Oh, the Señora. She is from Venezuela, originally, with all the pride of one from that nation. Her husband met and married her while he was on business in that country. She is devoted to her son, and worships the ground that he treads on. Some would call her love almost obsessive."

"You have no liking for her, then? Remember, you told me you would be frank with me."

Locke shrugged. "I have no special liking for her, it is true, but then I have no strong dislike of her, either. The reverse is not true. She sees me as a ne'er-do-well and wastrel, and the Epsom business only strengthened her feelings against me. She felt I had brought disgrace on the family name." He smiled ruefully. "If I am to look at myself and my actions, I suppose I must admit that there is a certain justice in her accusations."

"Let us return to that Epsom business, if you do not mind."

Locke shrugged. "It is in the past. I will talk about it if you wish, though I would prefer not to do so."

"What was your role in the business?"

"I was a medical student at Guy's for a number of years. Accordingly, I was deputed to administer a dose of opium to the favourite in the races on which the bets were to be laid."

"How was this to be administered?" I asked.

"I was to inject the horses with a hypodermic needle." He shuddered. "I am happy that I never had to perform the operation. I was confident enough in the dissecting room," he explained, "but the idea of inserting a knife or a needle into living flesh terrified me, and it was that, in fact, that caused me to give up the idea of medicine as a profession."

"And now work for Lightfoot & Co.?"

"Thanks to Earnest, yes. It is a relatively lowly position but it is a living, and there is room for promotion. I do not use Earnest's name to gain any advantages, and he has been scrupulous in not providing any such. I am very grateful to him for the post, as well as for his permitting me to live in his house as he does."

"Do you still correspond with those who were accused along with you?"

"Are you asking me if I still wager on the horses?" Locke smiled. "At least one of those accused with me was a good friend, and has remained a friend, through it all. Yes, I am in regular contact with two of these people, and yes, we visit the racecourses together from time to time. I have learned my lesson, I think, and my bets are small, and I ensure that I never wager more than I can afford to lose."

"An honest enough answer," said Holmes. "One last question before we join the ladies. Do you know the contents of Sir Earnest's will?"

"I have no idea. I would assume that the estate would pass to my sister in its entirety."

"You do not know if you stand to gain by his death?"

"I do not know. I would consider it to be extremely unlikely. Is he likely to die, do you think? I believed him to be merely sick."

"He is seriously ill," I said. "For a more detailed prognosis and diagnosis, you must consult Sir James Mackenzie."

"Let us join the ladies," Holmes said, rising.

I attempted to divert Lady Margaret's attention, but I fear I was sorry company for her. Holmes applied himself to old Mrs. Crosby, speaking in Spanish. Lady Margaret left us to visit her husband, and returned, red-eyed, a few minutes later.

"It is the end, Mama," she said to her mother-in-law. "I know it. You should make your farewells. You too, Thomas."

"Nonsense," said the old lady. "It is merely a touch of the fever that is going around. He will be better in the morning, you see." She made no move to stir from her chair. Thomas Locke appeared to be distraught. "I will go to him now, sister," he said softly, and slipped out of the room.

There was an embarrassed silence, broken only by the wheezing of a Pekinese that was sitting by the fire. I glanced at it, and Lady Margaret followed my gaze.

"Yes, poor little Pin-pon is all alone now. Chin-chon left us for a happier land about three months ago."

"I am sorry to hear that," I said.

"We have no idea what happened," she told me. "One morning we came down to breakfast, and there was poor little Chin-chon lying cold and stiff in his basket."

"He was old," said the old woman sharply, "and old dogs die."

"Yes, Mama," said Lady Margaret, and silence reigned once

more.

Suddenly, Lady Margaret stood up and shouted at the top of her voice, "I cannot abide this any longer!" and rushed out of the room, slamming the door behind her.

"Hysterical," commented the old lady.

I could not restrain myself any longer. "Madam," I said in as firm a tone as I could manage, "Lady Margaret's husband – your son – is possibly dying upstairs. Your attitude is markedly less than that I would expect from a woman of your breeding."

"We all get what we deserve," she retorted coldly. "And I do not ever remember being addressed like that in my own house, young man."

"I was not aware that it was your house," I answered hotly. "I was under the impression that it belonged to your son."

"I wish you a very good night, Mr. Holmes," she said in a frosty tone of voice, pointedly ignoring me, and rising.

Holmes refrained from reply, and remained seated, though she glared at him as if willing him to rise and open the door for her. At length she left us, opening the door herself.

I looked at Holmes, who was laughing silently.

"Bravo, Watson!" he said. "I will wager that no-one has spoken like that to that old dragon in decades. She deserved all that you said, and more."

"But what did she mean when she said that we all get what we deserve?"

"I wish I knew," he answered me.

"And what were you discussing with her?"

"I had to endure a long disquisition on the nobility of her family's antecedents. However, once we had put that behind us, she started to discourse on her other passion, which is natural history, specifically the flora and fauna of her native Venezuela. She claims to have reproduced some of the features of the country in the garden here in a caged-off area, and she offered to guide me around her creation tomorrow morning. I think," he chuckled, "that after tonight's exchange, you will not be included in the invitation."

"I believe I will find that no hardship," I answered.

A maid entered to take away the coffee cups.

"May I ask you a few questions?" Holmes asked her.

"If you must, sir. I have things to do, and Cook will be angry if I do not return to the kitchen soon."

"I will explain things to Cook if necessary," said Holmes, "and I will be as brief as possible. First, do Sir Earnest and Lady Margaret share a bedroom?"

"Lord bless you, no, sir. Not these last ten years or more. He sleeps in the room where he is now, if you know where that is, sir, and she sleeps at the other end of the passageway."

"And Mr. Thomas and Mrs. Crosby?"

Mr. Thomas has a small room and a sitting-room of his own on the floor above Sir Earnest and Lady Margaret. The old lady – beg pardon, sir – Mrs. Crosby, she sleeps in the room next to Sir Earnest that used to be the dressing-room when he and Lady Margaret both used the same bedroom."

"That is most interesting. Thank you very much. Oh, one last thing. I believe this is Pin-pon," gesturing to the Pekinese.

Her face softened. "Yes, sir. She misses Chin-chon still, though, sir. We all do."

"I had heard about that."

"It was me, sir, who discovered him. All cold and stiff he was in his little basket, sir."

"Tell me, did Mrs. Crosby have anything to do with the dogs?"

"Not as a rule, sir. She prefers the parrots and monkeys and things she keeps in the garden. But come to think of it, she started making a fuss of Chin-chon before he died. He was getting old, though, and he had trouble walking the past few weeks he was with us. Now if you'll excuse me, sir?"

"Of course. And here is half a sovereign for your help."

"Why, thank you, sir."

"What do we do now?" I asked when the maid had departed.

"We follow the example of the rest of the house. Sir James,

Lady Margaret, and Thomas Locke. We wait."

"And Mrs. Crosby?"

"She is also waiting – maybe for the same event, but for a different end."

The maid re-entered. "Sir James Mackenzie's compliments, Doctor Watson, but he would welcome your attendance at Sir Earnest's sickbed. You too, sir," addressing Sherlock Holmes.

I took up my medical bag and we hurried upstairs.

"It is a matter of minutes only," said Sir James. Mr. Holmes, I am sorry to ask you to do these things, but I would appreciate it if you could support the family when they arrive here. Watson, we are entering the stage of Cheyne-Stokes breathing pattern. I would be grateful for your assistance in making Sir Earnest's passage from this life as painless and as comfortable as possible."

I recognised the all-too-familiar breaths that are characteristic of those about to pass away, and, being all too familiar with death, was able to help Sir James in his work. There was none of the ill-temper about which I had been warned, and I saw tears in his eyes at more than one point as we carried out our duties. I was vaguely aware that Lady Margaret and her brother were in the room, but continued to administer what attentions I could.

At length, "It is over," said Sir James, and closed Sir Earnest's eyes.

Lady Margaret, weeping, bent to kiss her husband on the lips, and her brother reverently touched the dead man's forehead.

"But where is the mother?" asked Sir James in surprise.

"I do not think you will find her in this room tonight. At least, not when anyone else is in the chamber," Holmes told him quietly. Sir James looked at him sharply, but refrained from any questions.

"Come, Lady Margaret, and you, Locke. Assist your sister," Holmes said, as gently as I have ever heard him speak, offering his arm to the widow and leading her from the death-chamber.

He returned a few minutes later. "Her maid is taking care of her, and her brother is proving to be a tower of strength. Now, where is Sir Earnest's private correspondence? I would guess in this bureau here."

"You cannot do that," exclaimed Sir James, horrified, as Holmes bent to the desk in question.

"Believe me, Sir James, I do not do this lightly or for trivial reasons. You were Sir Earnest's friend, were you not?"

"I was."

"Treasure that friendship. I fear that if you were to see what I believe is in here, your faith in a good man might be shattered. Ah, this drawer is locked. No matter." He brought out his set of picklocks before the scandalised eyes of the physician. "Believe me, Sir James."

"If you find what you are seeking, I demand the right to see it for myself," replied the other. "I know of your reputation, but I do not feel that I can give you free rein to rifle my late friend's personal papers."

"You are sure?" asked Holmes, who by this time had opened the drawer.

"I am sure."

"Then here you are," said Holmes handing over a packet of papers tied with a pink ribbon. "As you can see, I have not even read them, but I know that these are what I have been seeking. There is a photograph, too." He handed it, unseen, to Sir James, who was examining the papers with a look of horror.

"I see what you are saying, Holmes. The existence of this woman and her children – good God! it seems that he actually married her." Sir James Mackenzie turned pale and sank into a chair. "You are right – the existence of these papers must never come to light. Take them and destroy them." He thrust the bundle back at Holmes, who secreted them in his breast pocket.

"I will do exactly that," said my friend, closing and re-locking the now-empty drawer where he had discovered the papers. "There is one last job to perform, and that is to catch the murderer. Watson has already told me of your suspicions – you know that Sir Earnest's death was not due to natural causes, whatever you may choose to write on the death certificate."

"Holmes, you frighten me beyond belief. I cannot countenance such doings."

"Nonetheless, will you do as I ask you for the rest of the night? For your friend, Sir James?"

The doctor looked at Holmes with a frightened gaze, and held out his hand, which Holmes grasped. "I do not know why I trust you, Holmes, but yes, I will do what you say."

"Good." Holmes raised his voice. "Let us leave Sir Earnest to his rest, and we shall mourn his memory downstairs."

"Yes, let us go," I said loudly, taking my cue from Holmes.

We left the room, Holmes and I making as much noise about the business as we could, and Sir James gamely joining, us, though with a bemused expression on his face.

"Now," whispered Holmes when we had reached the bottom of the stairs. "Remove your boots." He opened and closed the drawing-room door loudly before removing his own boots. "Up the stairs, as quietly as you can." He led the way back into the death chamber. "And now we wait," he whispered.

An hour passed, two hours. I heard the hall clock strike, and then. A gleam of light as the connecting door to the next room – the former dressing-room that was now the bedroom of the old harridan – was slowly and cautiously opened.

Holmes had positioned us so that we were invisible to anyone entering the room through that door, and so we were able to observe old Mrs. Crosby, muttering to herself, lamp in hand, as she made her way to the bureau. She inserted a key into the very drawer from which Holmes had removed the papers, which opened with a click.

On discovering the drawer was empty, she let out a snarl, more animal than human. Holmes stepped forward into the light of the lamp, and she let out a startled gasp.

"I have the papers," said Holmes.

"They are mine!" she hissed at him. "My son's, and therefore mine."

"You have forfeited all rights to motherhood. You lost them when you killed your son."

"What?" gasped Sir James.

"He deserved to die," she said. "No son of mine would bring dishonour to our family in that way. I demanded, time and again, that he break off his liaison with that woman, but he refused. There was only one path left for me to take, and I took it."

"But how did you extract the blood from Sir Earnest and introduce the poison into his system?" I asked.

"I did nothing of the sort," she replied. "I had assistance. Come, young man." As if hypnotised, I followed her beckoning finger, Holmes and Mackenzie in my wake as we passed through the connecting door.

"Look!" She flung wide a cabinet door, revealing a glass tank in which were suspended some loathsome red forms.

"The giant red leech of Venezuela," breathed Holmes. "*Hellobdella rufens gigans*. A leech that attacks its prey, not with jaws, but with a small needle-like proboscis, and a secretion that renders the skin porous, allowing a greater flow of blood, while injecting a poisonous drug into its victims."

"They are the only specimens in this country," the old lady told us proudly. "I applied them to Earnest as he slept, and retrieved them before he awoke, and before they could do any lasting damage. I warned him that if he did not mend his ways, he would die. He did not mend his ways. He died."

"And you, madam, will also die, but at the end of a rope," snarled Mackenzie.

"Not so," said the old woman, and thrust her bare arm into the tank, where a dozen of the repulsive creatures immediately fastened themselves to her. "This is painless. I shall no longer be with you in an hour or two..." Her voice trailed off, and she sank to the floor, the vile pulsating red lumps still attached to her arm.

"Shall we not save her?" asked Mackenzie.

"And bring the whole business before the public gaze? No, let us let her go her own way. It will be better. She is known for her love of exotic fauna. If some of them turn out to be dangerous – what is that to us?"

"Even so…" muttered Mackenzie, but he watched with Holmes and myself as the horrors sucked the life from the old woman.

The emotions roused in me as we observed the old woman slip away from us were mixed, and have never entirely left me. My natural humanity and my Hippocratic oath did battle with my disgust and hatred of the hag who was determined to cheat the hangman of his rightful due.

Before it was over, Holmes turned away. "Come," he ordered us, and we followed.

"It was elementary," said Holmes to me as we returned on the District Railway to Baker-street, back to the fogs of London. "Once it was clear that Sir Earnest's condition was not natural, Thomas was, of course, my first object of suspicion, but he soon cleared his name, as far as I am concerned, at any rate. The dog, of course, was the first experiment with the leeches, giving us the means, though I was unsure of the exact method she had used until I saw the leeches."

"You had heard of them?"

"I had read of them in a book written by a traveller to that region. They are reputed to be one of the greatest hazards to travellers in that area. A horse may die within the hour if enough of these vile monsters attack."

"The connecting door between Sir Earnest's room and that of his mother was a clear opportunity, of course, but how did you come to know that Sir Earnest had contracted a bigamous marriage? The motive for his mother's actions?"

"I had guessed that there was some shameful secret, when his mother made the comment about those who deserve to die, and from her comments about her family and her pride in it. I did not know what that secret might be, however, but was almost certain that if proof existed, it would be in the one locked drawer of the bureau. And so it was." We journeyed on in silence for a little while. "Well, Watson," he said smiling. "I now have to think how I shall report all this to Lestrade. Sir James and I must put our heads together on this."

"You would pervert the course of justice?"

"There are times when the justice as defined by our laws must be blind, in the interests of a higher Justice." And no more would he say on the matter.

# THE ADVENTURE
## OF THE ADDLETON
# TRAGEDY

R. HOLMES, it is essential that you come to Addleton immediately!" our fair visitor said to Sherlock Holmes. "Mamma will find it impossible to spend another night there unless we know the source of these goings-on."

Miss Edith Courtney, who addressed these words to my friend, the first since her greetings and introduction, was a handsome young lady, perhaps not twenty-five years of age. Her otherwise attractive face was marred by the lines of worry, and a haggard expression showed in her eyes. She had written to Sherlock Holmes announcing her intention to call on him the same afternoon, and she had presented herself at our door at precisely the time she had stated in the letter, smartly and fashionably dressed, and, despite her obvious concern, a quality of self-assurance about her.

"What goings-on are these?" Holmes asked her in answer to her demand.

"Why, the noises at night that keep her awake, and keep us shivering with fear in our beds. You must, must, must, return to Addleton with me this evening and help put our fears to rest." Her pale cheeks flushed with emotion as she made this earnest appeal to Holmes.

"Why, Miss Courtney, pray calm yourself and explain your troubles from the beginning."

"You have heard of Addleton, I take it?"

Holmes shook his head.

"Why, Mr. Holmes, what circles do you move in?"

"Those which I am sure are rather different to yours," smiled Holmes. "Tell me why I should have heard of Addleton."

It was I rather than Miss Courtney who answered him. "I was reading about it only last week in the *Illustrated London News*. Addleton is the name of a splendid old Jacobean house belonging to the Courtney family. Professor Courtney of the University of London is Miss Courtney's father, I believe?" Our visitor nodded. "He has recently become President of a learned society that interests itself in those phenomena that are inexplicable by modern science, such as communication through mental faculties alone, without speech, and the survival of personality after death."

"That is correct, Doctor," said Miss Courtney, "and it is the last of these that is causing concern. You are surely aware, Mr. Holmes, of the activities of those who call themselves 'Spiritualists', who believe that the spirits of the departed may be contacted and who can give us advice."

"Naturally I have heard of them," said Holmes.

"Your scepticism is evident in your voice," smiled our visitor. "I, too, was an unbeliever in these things until recently. My father, as you explained, Doctor, is interested in these phenomena. He has quite frequently invited the so-called mediums who profess to contact the departed spirits to our home. I have sat at some of the séances where the supposed powers of the people have been displayed. For the most part, they are sorry cheats, who seek to deceive the public in exchange for money. Those who have recently lost a loved one will often pay for a medium to speak to them in the voice of the dead."

"I have heard of this," I said.

"They play tricks with luminous paint, and so on. My father has exposed several of them in the most ludicrously fraudulent activities. It concerns me to know that there are those out there who will believe them. And yet..." Her voice tailed off.

"Pray continue," said Holmes.

"There are some mediums who have visited that not even my father can explain. While holding their hands, and restraining their feet, he has observed raps and bangs coming from other parts of the room. Sometimes they appear to have materialised spirits, who leave impressions of their hands in soft wax."

I was intrigued by this last. "But surely, if they are spirits, they cannot leave impressions?""

"I assure you, Doctor Watson, that I have seen such

impressions in wax, and furthermore, the cavities left by hands are larger than the diameter of the wrists, meaning that there is no way in which a human hand could have entered and left the wax. My father is at a loss as to how to explain this, as am I, of course."

"You have attended these sessions – these séances, I take it?"

"Many times. And now I am convinced that some of these people – not all, by any manner of means – have powers out of the ordinary. I am now even more convinced than I was, given the events of the past few days."

"Go on," urged Holmes. It was clear to me that, despite his scepticism regarding such happenings, he was keenly interested in the narrative that was unfolding before us.

"One of the world's foremost mediums visited us a little less than a week ago. She is Italian by birth, and came highly recommended by many. Her séance consisted of materialisations of faces and arms, the playing of a musical box which was placed in a locked box before the séance, and many raps and bangs from the furniture in the room. She spoke to me in the voice of my deceased grandmother of things that I believed were only known to me, and my father likewise received messages, apparently from beyond the grave, which astounded him."

"So in your opinion, this woman is genuine?"

"Whether she is communicating with spirits, I do not know, but she certainly seems to have powers beyond the natural. However, that is not what is concerning me and my mother. The medium departed, having been paid well for her trouble, but that night, I was awakened at a quarter past two in the morning by a loud thumping sound."

"You seem very sure of the time, Miss Courtney."

She smiled. "I am the daughter of a scientist, and he has trained me in observation and accuracy from the time I was a girl."

"Excellent. Proceed."

"At first I thought it must be coming from outside the house. Perhaps, I considered, a horse in the stables was kicking at the stalls, or some such, but when I got up from my bed and listened by the window, it seemed to be coming from inside the house. I put on my dressing-gown, and walked out onto the landing, but was unable to ascertain the source of the noises, and therefore returned to my room."

"Can you describe the noise?"

"A hollow thumping booming sound, at reasonably regular intervals of between ten and fifteen seconds. The sounds – it is hard to describe them accurately, but if I give you the fanciful description of a giant striking the top of a large empty barrel with a club, you will have some idea of what I experienced."

"And for how long did these noises continue?"

"For fifteen minutes after they started. I went back to sleep, and was awakened at quarter to five in the morning by the noise once more. There was a little more light, and I arose instantly to investigate. I determined that the sound was emanating from one of the bedrooms that is reserved for guests – the medium had used it when she spent the night following the séance. However, there were no guests staying with us of whom I was aware, and I could not for the life of me imagine what was causing the sounds. Maybe, I considered, one of the servants might be performing some household chore, though it was hard for me to imagine what manner of work it might be, and why it should be performed at that hour."

"Quite so," murmured Holmes.

"I therefore opened the door to the bedroom, but it was empty. The knocking sound boomed out, and I confess, Mr. Holmes, I was afraid. I consider myself to be a rational person, but this sent a shiver down my spine. I rushed out of the room and slammed the door shut. Immediately, the noises stopped, and the sudden silence was more terrifying than the sound had been. Something was listening and watching me, I felt sure, and this knowledge frightened me."

"This seems most understandable," I consoled her.

"I went back to bed, but this time I could not sleep. I lay under the bedclothes, literally shivering with fear. At breakfast the next morning, my mother asked me if I had heard anything, and I told her what had transpired the previous night."

"And your father?"

"He was in London that night. He often spends the night there after attending lectures and so on."

"Other than the servants, only your mother and you were in the house?"

"My mother's father, who lives with us."

"And the reaction of your mother and your grandfather?"

"My mother was terrified by what I related, more so than me. My grandfather is hard of hearing, and told us that he had heard nothing, sleeping soundly through the whole night."

"And the servants?"

"I personally questioned the servants, as my mother seemed to be in no fit state to do so. They had heard the noises, but they sleep in a wing of the house far from the room from where the noise was coming, and they assumed the sound was coming from outside the house. None admitted to having entered the room since the departure of our last guest, the Italian medium."

"Have there been any other manifestations? Has anything been observed by any members of the household? Any furniture moved around by unseen hands, for example?"

"Nothing, unless you count the disappearance of two large cooking pans from the kitchen a few days ago. Cook was most vexed at their disappearance and complained to me about them." She paused, and regarded Holmes quizzically. "I do believe you are mocking me. I take it you do not believe in these matters, Mr. Holmes?"

"I am by no means mocking you, Miss Courtney, merely attempting to ascertain the facts of the case, and to determine whether there is anything in common with what I have heard in the past, though I admit that I find it hard to credit some of the stories I have been told," answered Holmes. "Though I do not believe most of these tales, I attempt to maintain an open mind and, should the evidence admit of no other explanation, then, as I have previously remarked to Watson, when the impossible has been eliminated, whatever remains, however improbable it may seem, must stand as the truth."

"So you believe that these sounds have a natural explanation?"

"Without knowing more of the facts, I believe that to be so. Was the instance which you have just related the only occasion they have occurred?"

"These sounds have repeated themselves on the two nights succeeding – that is to say, last night and the night before that."

"At the same times?"

"Approximately so. That is to say, within thirty minutes of the times that they first occurred."

"And they seemed to appear from the same source?"

"Yes, they came from the empty room. Last night, I heard the booming sounds once again, and I threw on my dressing-gown and made immediately for the source of the noises. They stopped almost immediately after I had opened the door, but instead of leaving the room, I sat in the chair by the bed and waited for the sounds to begin again."

"That must have taken considerable courage," I remarked.

She smiled faintly. "I confess that I was extremely frightened of what might occur. Though it was late, and I was tired, I found it impossible to close my eyes. I had my watch with me, and accordingly I was able to ascertain the hour at which they started again." Here her eyes grew wide, as she appeared to relive the events of the night before. "The sounds were almost deafening, and appeared to come from all around me. There was no single source that I was able to identify."

"What did you do?"

"I fled, Mr. Holmes, I confess it. I flung the door wide, and raced to the safety of my room." She paused.

"There is more?"

"Yes. As I fled, I swear that I heard behind me the sound of mocking laughter, which did not appear to come from a human throat. The next morning, my mother asked me if I had heard the sounds. I told her that I had, but did not inform her of my nocturnal adventure, fearing that this would disturb her unnecessarily."

"Was it your idea to consult me?"

"Yes, it was at my own suggestion that I have made my way to you. While my father is away attending some sort of meeting for a few days, I have taken it upon myself to fill his place. My mother is not very strong, and it is my responsibility to make decisions in my father's absence."

"This is not my usual line of work, as you may be aware." Holmes regarded her keenly. "My business is with criminals rather than ghosts, as I am sure you are aware. The supernatural is beyond me, I fear."

"I beg you, Mr. Holmes, if not for my sake, then for that of my mother, make your way to Addleton and assure my mother that these sounds have a natural and not a supernatural cause, and that you will attempt to discover these causes? Even if you cannot ascertain the true facts, your presence alone will reassure her."

"Tell me," I interrupted, "if there is any legend attached to the house that might appear to her to be a cause of supernatural manifestations."

To my surprise, she gave a gay laugh. "There is indeed. There is a story that in the conflict between the Royalists and the Parliamentarians, one of the King's chief advisers took refuge with the family then resident in the house. There was a hidden room – legend has it that it was a priest's hole – in which the family concealed him when the Roundheads came searching. They were unable to discover him, but took away the family for questioning. The hidden room could not be opened from the inside, and in the time that the family was detained by the Parliamentarians, the unfortunate Cavalier starved to death. His spirit is popularly supposed to haunt the house."

"A grisly tale," I commented.

"Indeed. It may well be a true history. My father and I consider the story of the ghost to be nonsense, however. No member of our family, and none of the servants report having seen it at any time."

"And your mother?" Holmes enquired sharply. "Does she believe in the reality of this spirit?"

"You have put your finger on it, Mr. Holmes. My mother is most certainly aware of the legend, and believes it to be the source of these mysterious knockings. The spirit of the unfortunate nobleman who died in the hidden room has been awakened by Signora Patroni, she feels."

"And you, yourself?"

Our fair visitor shrugged. "My father has taught me to keep an open mind on these matters, while at the same time always keeping in mind the likelihood of a natural explanation. It is true that Signora Patroni produced effects that I have never before experienced at a séance, and which I find it hard to ascribe to the tricks of a conjuror. However, at no point did she mention the legend, let alone make any claims to be in contact with this spirit that is supposed to haunt the house. I admit that I am frightened, Mr. Holmes, but I am unsure of exactly what I am frightened."

"That seems a reasonable answer." Holmes paused to consider for the space of about half a minute. "Despite my earlier words, this case would appear to have some interest. Watson, be so good as to look in Bradshaw and find out the next train that will take us both to Addleton with our client."

It was typical of Holmes that he neglected to enquire of me as to my availability. I said nothing, however, and reached for the volume in question, but was pre-empted by a smiling Miss Courtney, who held out a sheet of paper to Holmes.

"I had hoped you would agree to make the visit," she explained, "and therefore prepared this list of possible trains."

"Capital!" exclaimed Holmes. "You are clearly a person of

considerable foresight and resource."

On the train to the Oxfordshire countryside, we passed the time conversing with Miss Courtney about her father's interest in the psychic phenomena that she had described, and the work he had done to establish or disprove the authenticity of these things. Though I knew little about the subject, by the time she had finished describing the experiments and the research conducted by her father and her friends, I was convinced that if such phenomena actually took place, then these were the people who would confirm their existence through clear scientific means. Holmes, for his part, maintained a detached silence, though it was clear from his face that he was following the thread of the conversation.

We alighted at the station that served the house, and hired the services of a dog-cart to take us to Addleton itself, some two miles away. However, Holmes declared that he was in need of exercise and would sooner walk, and after receiving directions from Miss Courtney, strode off towards the house.

I, for my part, was only too happy to continue in the company of this charming and intelligent young lady, and the short distance was covered quickly – perhaps too quickly for my liking.

Mrs. Courtney received us in the drawing-room, and greeted me. She was a woman who had once obviously been beautiful, and traces of that beauty still remained in her face, but she appeared to lack the spirit which animated her daughter.

"I am so glad that you have come, Mr. Holmes," she said to me. "I trust that you will be able to provide us with a satisfactory answer as to the dreadful goings-on that my daughter has told you of."

"I am not Sherlock Holmes," I replied, laughing. "He will be with us shortly." I introduced myself, and explained Holmes' preference to walk rather than to take the cart. "However," I continued, "I may well be able to provide some assistance of my own."

"Edith," her mother told Miss Courtney. "When Doctor

Watson has been shown to his room, perhaps you would be good enough to let him see the priest's hole."

"It is still in existence, then?"

"It forms one of the attractions of the house," Miss Courtney replied, smiling.

The room which Holmes and I were to occupy was a noble chamber, with oak panelled walls, and heavy hangings over the leaded windows. As I washed my hands and face at the washstand, I espied Holmes walking up the drive towards the house. I therefore expected the doorbell to ring in a matter of a minute or so, but I judged it to be a matter of some ten minutes before I heard the sound of the bell, and the door being opened to admit my friend. He entered the room, shortly afterwards, smiling.

"Well, Watson," he exclaimed, looking around the room. "We seem to be placed in the lap of Jacobean luxury, do we not?" He strode to one of the panels beside the fireplace, and rapped smartly upon it with his knuckles. It emitted a hollow sound, albeit faint.

"You believe that is the source of the noises that have upset the family?" I asked.

"I hardly think this noise would cause the worry and fear that have been described to us."

There was a knock at the door, which startled me, coming as hard upon the heels of Holmes' knocking as it did.

We opened the door to disclose Miss Courtney, who invited us to view the priest's hole. "I will lead you there," she smiled.

"No need," Holmes told her. "I will take you to the place." To my astonishment, and that of Edith Courtney, he led the way along a passageway, and down a short flight of steps, before stopping before a panelled wall. "Here, I believe."

"Why, Mr. Holmes, you are a magician!" she exclaimed. "Next, you will tell me how to open the door, I am sure."

"I do not know with any certainty, but I can attempt to discover the secret," he answered her. His hands moved to the moulded beading surrounding the panel, and his long sensitive fingers played over it. "Aha!" he exclaimed. As he pushed on a part of the moulding, it swivelled about its axis. He then proceeded to slide the panel sideways to reveal a small room, faintly lit by a slit window that was similar in size and shape to other windows let into the walls of the hallway, staircase, and landing.

"How on earth..?" I asked him.

Holmes smiled, but gave no answer.

"Since you have discovered it with so little effort, you should be the first to enter it," Edith Courtney invited him.

He stepped through the opening, stooping as he did so, and I followed. The chamber in which we found ourselves was about six feet in length, and three in width. The ceiling was some five feet above the floor, forcing us both to bend uncomfortably, and the walls were of stone. Holmes rapped at them, as well as at the ceiling and the floor, with the end of his stick, but the walls appeared to be solid and there were no sounds produced such as had been described to us. Even tapping at the panel that served the narrow space as a door failed to produce the booming resonance that Miss Courtney told us that she had experienced.

"Thank goodness for the window," I remarked. "I truly believe I would develop symptoms of madness were I to be confined in such a small space without access to the outside world."

"I agree," said Holmes, as he and I exited the confined space. "Does the legend tell us how long the poor unfortunate was confined before he perished?" he asked.

"We are told it was a matter of some three weeks."

I shuddered. "The poor man," I said.

"His body was removed and buried secretly in the churchyard, and a memorial tablet placed in the parish church after the Restoration. You may see it, if you like."

"I have my doubts as to whether it will aid us in solving this mystery," said Holmes. "I do not think that the priest's hole is connected with the sounds you described. The walls and floor appear to be solid, as does the door. I see no way in which the sounds could be created from here."

"Then I will take you to the room from which the sounds appeared to come."

"First, though, I would like to know the location of your bed-room."

For answer, she pointed to one of the doors leading from the landing.

"And that of your mother?"

She pointed three doors along the passageway.

"The servants' rooms are in the other wing, you say? On the floor above this?"

"Indeed so."

"And the guest room from which you perceived the sounds?"

"This one." She stopped in front of a door opposite that which she had indicated as hers, at the other end of the passageway.

Holmes paused, his hand on the door handle. "It is locked?"

"No, the doors in this house are never locked."

We entered the room, and I could not help but utter an exclamation of delight at what I saw there. A large hooded fireplace, surmounted by an intricately carved oaken mantel, formed the main feature of the room. "Surely that is the work of Grinling Gibbons?" I asked.

Our fair guide smiled in response. "It is indeed, and it was created at the same time as the monument to the unfortunate Cavalier in the church, which is also said to be by him."

I examined the carving, which was a true masterpiece of its kind, with the skill of the artist who created it evident in every minute detail.

Holmes, for his part, seemed indifferent to the beauties of the mantel, and seemed to be concentrating on the fireplace and chimney itself.

"What is below here?" he asked. "Which room?"

"Why, it is the one in which Grandfather sleeps. He is elderly, and it is a sore trial for him to go up and down stairs at his age."

"And yet he heard nothing, you say?"

"He is very hard of hearing. Without his ear-trumpet, it is very difficult to make him understand anything that is said to him. It is perfectly possible for him to sleep through a thunderstorm – and that is no figure of speech – he has often been unaware of the most violent tempests that have blown up in the night. You will have the pleasure of his company this evening at dinner." There was a faint rueful smile on her face as she pronounced these last words.

"I believe you are not telling us all, Miss Courtney," Holmes admonished her.

For answer, she blushed a little and started to stammer. "He is not always the most pleasing of company. It seems that there is little in this world that pleases him in his old age, and much that vexes him. He makes his displeasure at the world obvious to all, at some length. And because he is unable to hear our pleas to stop his complaining, this may continue for a long time." She sighed. "Indeed, although he is her father, Mamma has considered the possibility that he no longer lodge with us, but that he live with my uncle in Walthamstow, or take up residence in another building on the estate."

"And your father?"

She smiled ruefully. "He would never admit it to me or my mother, but I have a suspicion that my grandfather is one of the reasons why my father spends so many nights away from this house."

Holmes bent to the fireplace once more, and appeared to be examining the back of the hearth. "Would you know when the fires were last lit in this room, or in your grandfather's room?"

"Let me think. It is now July, and this spring was a warm one. I would say that there has been no fire lit in this room for at least two months. My grandfather appears not to feel the cold, and it is unlikely that a fire has been lit in his room."

"And the chimneys have not been swept since that time?"

"I would have little idea of that, Mr. Holmes. You would have to ask the housekeeper."

"Of course." Holmes appeared a little abashed. "And likewise, you would have no idea whether starlings or other birds nest in the chimneys?"

"Really, Mr. Holmes!" she laughed. "What questions you ask, to be sure. No, I have no idea."

"Perhaps you would be kind enough to introduce me to the housekeeper?" said Holmes.

"Of course, if you feel that this will be germane to your enquiries."

"Indeed it will."

Mrs. Huxtable, the housekeeper, was a genial soul, and was obviously thrilled to be speaking with Sherlock Holmes.

"I've seen your name in the papers often enough, sir," she told him, "but I never thought I'd be helping you with a case." She giggled, almost girlishly, as Sherlock Holmes examined her, gravely.

"You seem like a sensible woman, Mrs. Huxtable, and I hope that you will be able to answer some simple questions."

"Is this about the noises that Miss Edith and the mistress say they've been hearing?"

"Precisely, Mrs. Huxtable. I knew you were an intelligent woman." She flushed with pride. "Now, what I would like to know is when the chimney in the guest bedroom and the old man's bedroom were last swept."

"Well, those two rooms share a chimney, as I suppose a man like you has already noticed. But they haven't been swept this year. We usually have the chimneys swept in August or early September, before we start lighting the fires for the winter."

"That seems a very sensible way of doing things. And you find you have no trouble with birds nesting in the chimneys?"

"Why, no, sir. Perkins, the gamekeeper, would make sure of that."

"And you have never heard these noises?"

"I wouldn't go so far as to say that, sir. I heard them last night, but they weren't loud enough to wake me up. I had gone to bed early, and woken up. I lit the lamp, and I was reading a few pages before I went back to sleep again—"

"What were you reading?" Holmes interrupted.

"It was some sort of romance, sir," she answered, somewhat embarrassed.

"What time was this?"

"A quarter past two by my alarm clock."

"That corresponds to the time we were told earlier," Holmes remarked to me. "And what did you think?" he asked Mrs. Huxtable.

"I thought it was a horse or something outside the house. It wasn't loud enough to bother me."

"You didn't consider that it might be a ghost or something along those lines?" Holmes asked her.

She laughed heartily. "Bless you, sir, the master may play around with his spooks and his spirits. I don't hold with it, myself. Not that I believe in any of it, you understand, but just in case they do exist, it's probably not a good idea to play around with them like that, wouldn't you say, sir?"

"I would agree that is a sensible line to take with regard to these matters," Holmes agreed gravely. "And the old story about the man who died in the priest's hole?"

"Well, that happened hundreds of years ago, didn't it, sir? No point in my troubling myself about it now, is there?"

"Quite. Have any of the servants been worried by these noises?"

She thought for a moment before replying. "Well, there's Jane, the scullery-maid, who threatened to leave us on account of them, but she's a bit simple, begging your pardon, sir. There was a mouse in the pantry a few weeks ago, and she wouldn't go anywhere the place for a few days, even though Perkins trapped it most neatly and showed her that there was nothing to worry about. Mind you, she never heard the noises herself. It was only me who did that. Jane only heard of the noises from me, and she went all historical." I smiled to myself at this last.

"Thank you, Mrs. Huxtable, you have been of great assistance to us," Holmes informed her.

"My pleasure, sir," she answered.

"Well, Watson, what do you make of it so far?" he asked me, as we walked along the passageway to the drawing-room.

"I am astounded by the way in which you located the hidden room," I told him.

"Oh, that was a mere matter of walking around the outside of the house and counting the windows. There were three of those slit windows visible from the outside, but there were only two opening from the staircase, as I am sure you observed. It was a simple matter to locate the approximate area in which the hidden room was to be found, and then equally trivial to locate the opening. I have had some experience in these matters, as you are aware, and indeed, have made a small contribution to the subject in the form of a monograph published in the *Architect's Gazette*."

"Even so, it was an impressive feat. Our hostess was visibly astounded."

Holmes smiled. "Such little tricks are more striking if their secrets are not revealed, are they not? Is there anything else that strikes you?"

"You have clearly discovered something of interest in the chimney of that room, though I could not determine for myself what it was."

"Indeed, I believe the answer to the mystery is far from being the result of supernatural causes, and lies in that chimney."

We returned to our room and dressed for dinner before proceeding downstairs to the drawing-room, where we encountered old Mr. Lymington, the grandfather.

My first impression of him was not a favourable one. His appearance was unkempt, and, as we had been warned, he was extremely hard of hearing, and he flourished a large ear-trumpet, seemingly at will. On being introduced to me, he barked stiffly, "Doctor, eh? Who said I need a doctor, then, eh?" he fairly bellowed at me.

With some difficulty I was able to explain to him that I was not visiting in any medical capacity, but in my role as the colleague of Sherlock Holmes, but this explanation did not appear to please him any better than the previous one.

"Stuff and nonsense!" he roared. "I'd face twenty ghosts a night and give them what-for! Foolish women's fancies," he added, glaring at his daughter and granddaughter. "As long as I am in the house, there is no danger. If I were not here, of course, there is no knowing what might take place."

The meal was an uncomfortable one. Old Mr. Lymington treated us throughout the soup and the fish courses to his views on the Jews, who were in his opinion, responsible for the troubles afflicting the modern world. His wild slanders were hateful to any man of sense and decency, and it was with some difficulty that I held my peace.

Sherlock Holmes, however, who numbered several of the Jewish race among his few friends, had less patience than did I. "Upon my word, sir," he fairly exploded, after one particularly poisonous accusation. "You are talking of a race among whom there are many whom I respect and think highly of. Such unsupported accusations that you have been making are unworthy of an English gentleman."

I truly believed the old man would fall over from apoplexy. His face turned brick red, and then purple, and he sputtered with rage. "I never thought to hear such words from a guest in my house," he spat out at length.

"And for my part, I never thought to enter a house where such thoughts were voiced by my host," retorted Holmes.

The two glared at each other in what appeared to be mutual loathing and disdain for the other. Neither spoke for some time, and then each bent to his plate in silence.

The rest of the meal was served in a stony silence, and as soon as he had finished his dessert, Lymington announced that he was going straight to bed.

"I am sorry about my father," Mrs. Courtney said to us. "He has become increasingly – shall we say, difficult? – in the past few years. I am sorry that my husband is still in London, as my father does not behave like this when he is here. To be frank, I have expressed the view that he should no longer remain with us. Although he is my father, his temperament and his views are at odds with a calm household. Several of the servants have given notice recently, and informed me that they found it impossible to live in the same house as him."

Her daughter broke in. "He is definitely a trial to us, and we have several times suggested to him that he move to the gatekeeper's lodge at the bottom of the drive and set up his household here, where he would be less of a burden to us, but we would be within easy call, should that be necessary. Alternatively, as I mentioned, he might lodge with my uncle in Walthamstow."

Mrs. Courtney nodded, and smiled, though nervously, her manner betraying an underlying nervousness and hesitancy as she addressed us. "But this is enough about our worries, which are surely of no interest to you, Mr. Holmes and Doctor Watson. Please feel free to stay in this room and smoke a cigar before joining my daughter and me," she invited. "The port is said by my husband and his colleagues to be drinkable," she smiled.

"Thank you, but no," Holmes answered her. "I would much prefer your company and that of your daughter. I see enough of Watson at other times," he smiled. "Let us leave the table together."

We rose, and our hostess led the way to the drawing-room, where we were served with our coffee and Holmes gradually led the subject of the conversation to the experiments and séances performed by her husband.

"I know that Charles – that is, my husband – insists that they are physical phenomena, and that there is nothing of the supernatural about them," she said, "but I cannot help but believe in the spirits that these mediums claim to be contacting. What is your opinion, Mr. Holmes, and yours, Doctor Watson?"

"I believe," he answered her, "along with your husband, that these phenomena have natural causes in most, if not in all, instances. However, should I come across a case where there was no obvious physical cause, I would be forced to reconsider my opinion."

"You will remain awake tonight, though?" she enquired, a trifle anxiously. "It will set my mind at rest to know that you will be in the house should the noises reoccur."

"My dear Mrs. Courtney," Holmes assured her, "Doctor Watson and myself will be ready for whatever may be causing these sounds. Indeed, we will spend the night in the room from which your daughter has informed us that the sounds emanate, rather than the splendid room that has been prepared for us."

I looked at him sharply, and I fancied I caught a glance of admiration from Miss Courtney, but Holmes was apparently oblivious of the attention.

After a little more conversation, we took ourselves upstairs to the bed-room, and I questioned Holmes.

"We are unarmed," I told Holmes, "and supposing these sounds to have a natural cause, should we not be prepared to meet an adversary?"

Holmes smiled. "If my deductions are correct, there is no need for us to defend ourselves."

"You surely do not believe that these sounds have a supernatural original?" I asked him, incredulously.

"By no means. However, I believe these will be of use," he went on, taking a pair of dark-lanterns from his travelling-bag. "Come, let us take up our positions."

We made our way to the "haunted" chamber, where we settled ourselves in the armchairs. It was a long wait in the dark, and my nerves were strained almost to breaking point, despite Holmes' calm assurance that there was nothing of the supernatural in the sounds that had been heard. We could hear the clock in the stable-yard strike the quarter hours regularly, until I was able to count the twelve strokes of midnight.

"This would seem to be a suitable time to prepare the lanterns," said Holmes as the echoes of the clock died away. A match flared as he lit both lanterns. He closed the shutters on the lanterns, and the room became dark again, the smell of hot metal becoming apparent as he handed one of the lanterns to me.

From that point, the stable clock appeared to stop striking, and I guessed that an hour had passed. Despite my worry, I was drowsy. Indeed, I believe that I had actually drifted off to sleep when I was startled by a loud booming noise which appeared to come from all around us, as had been described by Miss Courtney. The sound was repeated at intervals of about ten seconds, and the relative silence between each stroke, in which the anticipation of the next grew, was almost more terrifying than the sounds themselves.

"Where is this all coming from?" I whispered to Holmes, though in truth there was little cause for me to lower my voice.

"It is hard to tell from the sound alone," he replied, in his normal voice, "but I am convinced that its source is the fireplace."

I concentrated on the sound, but was unable to determine the location of the sound with any accuracy.

"Let us make our way downstairs," Holmes said to me. "We must exercise the utmost caution and stealth as we do so."

He moved noiselessly to the door, and opened it slowly. I followed him, the booming knocks following us as we made our way down the stairs to the entrance of the room where we had been told that old Mr. Lymington slept. A faint light showed under the door. "As I thought," Holmes breathed to me almost silently.

With a sudden movement, he threw open the door, and flung open the shutter of his dark-lantern, flooding the room with light. I followed, and beheld a strange scene.

Lymington was seated by the fireplace, seemingly unaware of our intrusion, and manipulating a cord that appeared to lead up the chimney. As he pulled at the cord, the booming sound sounded from above, and the old man gave a hideous, albeit almost noiseless, cackle and grinned horribly.

Holmes stepped forward, and laid a hand on the other's shoulder. Lymington's hand fell from the rope, and he started, gazing at Holmes' stern face with an air of terror.

"I see it all now," Sherlock Holmes said to him.

"Only my little joke, Mr. Holmes," whined the old man. "Only a joke."

"Hardly that, Mr. Lymington. Your object was to frighten the household, was it not, by manipulating the cooking utensils you abstracted from the kitchen and subsequently placed up the chimney to cause these noises that reverberated through the chimneys and the hollow double walls of this older part of the house."

"To what purpose would he do this?" I asked.

"Why, to ensure that he was not sent away from the house, of course. I am sure that even his own daughter would be glad if he were to live elsewhere. He hears us well enough, you see, even without his ear-trumpet," indicating the old man's face, which clearly showed that he was fully cognisant of what Holmes had been saying.

"They hate me, you know, because I tell the truth," spat out the old man. "The truth about those who wish to destroy our society and bring it down to their level. That is the reason they wish to put me in a place away from them, where they will not hear the things that make them uncomfortable, because they are true. True, I tell you!" he shrieked at us.

"I refuse to listen to your wild and hate-filled accusations," Holmes told him calmly.

"Why, you— you are as blind as the rest of them! They told me you were a clever man, Mr. Holmes, but they were wrong. You cannot or will not see what is in front of your very eyes!" He gesticulated wildly, sweeping his hand through the air, and knocked Holmes' dark-lantern from his hand. It fell on the chair where he was sitting, and the oil spilled from it.

In an instant, the flame from the lantern licked at the oil, and the chair was ablaze. There was a shrill scream from the old man, and I perceived with horror that his dressing-gown was on fire.

In an instant, I had stripped off my jacket, and smothered the flames, but the old man appeared to have lost consciousness. His breathing was rapid and shallow, and on my examining his pulse, his heartbeat appeared to be faint and irregular.

"How is he?" my friend asked me. "I am sure that he is untouched by the flames, since you acted with such commendable promptitude."

"He is in shock," I told Holmes. "I fear that at his age and in his state of health, the fear of the fire may prove as fatal as the fire itself."

"Quick! Hide the lanterns," Holmes told me. "I hear footsteps approaching."

An instant later, before we had time to conceal our lanterns, Edith Courtney entered the room. "Grandfather!" she exclaimed on seeing the unmoving form in the chair. "And..?" she added, puzzled, turning to Holmes and myself.

"We heard the noises," explained Holmes, "and came downstairs to investigate. We discovered your grandfather in this chair. He noted our presence, and turned to see us, and knocked over my lantern, which then set fire to the chair in which he is sitting. He appears to be unhurt, but Watson feels he may be in shock."

"He is sinking fast," I told her. "You may want to fetch your mother."

She left the room at a near-run. "He may not live to the morning. You did well in not exposing his ravings any further," I said to Holmes.

"She should not think of his last moments as those of a hate-filled monster," he answered me.

I add this little exchange to correct the ideas of those who may somehow have gained the impression that Sherlock Holmes was no more than a cold, calculating machine-like intelligence. To be sure, that is the way in which he preferred to see himself, and the guise in which he liked to present himself to the world, but to one who knew him as intimately as I, it was clear that a warm heart beat beneath the cold exterior shell.

There is little more to relate. In the interval between Miss Courtney's departure from the room, and her return with her mother, Holmes removed and concealed the cord that had been used to manipulate the kitchen utensils. Old Mr. Lymington died, as I had predicted, before the dawn broke, but I noted that neither his daughter nor grand-daughter seemed unduly distressed by his passing.

"And the noises?" asked Mrs. Courtney of Holmes.

"I believe they may somehow have been connected with your father. I feel it would be pointless to investigate further."

And so we took our leave of the Courtneys and Addleton, but not before Holmes had surreptitiously removed from the chimney the ingeniously fashioned apparatus which Lymington had used to create the sounds intended to terrify his family into allowing him to stay with him.

"A tragedy," said Holmes, as the train returning us to London pulled out of the village station.

"Indeed," I replied with feeling. "To die in such a fashion."

Holmes shook his head. "That was not the tragedy to which I was referring. I was speaking of the tragic waste of a mind that had sunk into those insane delusions that he expressed to us. Imagine the horror, Watson, should a whole nation ever think that way. For one man to think that way is a tragedy – if a whole population were to do so..." He shook his head sadly as we left the scene of the Addleton tragedy – however that term may be interpreted.

# The Adventure
## of the Ancient
## British Barrow

HERLOCK HOLMES, as I have mentioned many times in my accounts of his adventures, was a man of many talents in addition to those he displayed in his avocation of consulting detective. I have had occasion to remark his skill as a performer on the violin, as well as being a composer of no mean merit. His facility with the most abstruse chemical compounds would have gained him a Chair in the subject at any university, and his taste in wines, though I have had few occasions to remark it, was exquisite.

However, it is hard for a man of his intellectual capacity to be completely satisfied with one or two subjects, and he seemed constantly to be searching for new strings to add to his bow.

"My mind, Watson," he remarked to me once, "requires constant feeding and stimulation, or it will seize up, like a machine which is left unused and rusts in idleness. For all men, these things are desirable, but for me, they are a necessity."

It came as little surprise to me, therefore, when I entered the rooms in Baker-street one afternoon to discover my friend lying at full length on the floor, examining a large-scale map of East Anglia with his lens. Several volumes dealing with the Anglo-Saxon period were strewn around the room.

"It is significant, is it not, Watson, that although the majority of significant discoveries of Anglo-Saxon treasure have been made in this area, few of them have contained the golden ornaments that one would have expected to find in the tombs?"

"I had always understood that the Saxons were of a warlike and roving nature, and cared little for such frivolities," I answered him.

"I believe that view to be mistaken. Evidence is coming to light that, far from being the savages that we have always assumed, the Saxons were capable of appreciating and creating beauty, and were no strangers to the love of gold."

I laughed. "Have the criminals of the land been so

neglectful of their profession as to drive you to the distant past?"

"It is true," Holmes confessed, "that the London criminal, though he has not been idle of late, has nonetheless failed to show any originality in his operations. Why, even Lestrade and his myrmidons can solve the elementary puzzles set before them. My services are not in demand."

"And there are no private clients?" I asked him.

He sighed. "The Season has yet to start, and those clients who present themselves from that sector seem disinclined to visit London. As to the more humble of my clients, I fear that they likewise suffer from an astonishing lack of originality in their problems. I refuse to squander my talents on missing puppies or straying husbands. Therefore," and he turned to the map, "I engage my intelligence on this."

"And have you a problem to solve in this area of Anglo-Saxon antiquities?"

"I believe I have," he answered me, his eyes shining. "See here." He retrieved a sheet of paper from under one of the books, and passed it to me.

"Why, it is from Professor Harrington, the archeologist," I exclaimed. "He thanks you for your assistance in clearing up a mystery."

"Pah! It was nothing. Harrington has spent too many hours in the groves of Academe, and not enough in the world of the criminal classes. I was easily able to ascertain, from an examination of the skeleton, that the wounds inflicted on some unfortunate of the Anglo-Saxon era would have proved to be instantly fatal."

"And he invites you to participate in the excavation of a barrow near a place by the name of Little Melford. The name rings a bell, I fancy."

"Naturally it does. It is the village that was in the news some years back regarding a series of unsolved crimes."

"Why, so it was. I cannot recall the details, but I seem to remember that the police were baffled. Why were you not called in on that occasion?"

Holmes shrugged. "The local constabulary believed there was no need for my services. In any case, as you will remember, I was otherwise engaged at the time on the mystery of the Boscombe Valley. In any case, would you care to accompany me to Suffolk? I fancy you have been looking somewhat pale and out of sorts recently."

I laughed. "I am no such thing, Holmes, though I would certainly welcome the change. My practice is none too absorbing at present – I fear my patients, like your clients, are singularly unoriginal in their complaints – and it would be a positive pleasure to observe you at work on mysteries of a kind other than criminal."

"So be it. I will meet you at Liverpool-street Station at half-past eight tomorrow morning. I have already purchased two first-class tickets to Ipswich, from which we can take a carriage to Little Melford, where Harrington is staying together with his colleagues and assistants. He describes the barrow, I may tell you, as being one of the most promising he has yet encountered, if external signs are anything to go by."

"So be it. For how many days do you intend us to stay?"

"Four or five, unless there is an urgent summons from London. Mrs. Hudson has orders to refer any queries by potential clients to Little Melford by telegraph."

The next morning saw us traversing the flat Suffolk countryside in a dog-cart which we had hired at Ipswich station. Holmes was in an expansive mood, displaying his knowledge of medieval ecclesiastical architecture as we passed the fine churches, with their spires pointing to heaven, and built by the wool merchants who had become prosperous selling English fleeces to the Low Countries at that time.

Eventually we arrived at Little Melford. The house where we were to stay was a fine example of a dwelling of the sixteenth century, with half-timbering criss-crossing its white walls, and with honeysuckle in bloom framing its door and windows.

"A charming spot," I remarked, stretching and breathing in the country air.

"You know my views on the countryside," Holmes replied. "I truly believe that there is more hidden vice and wickedness in these charming villages than there is in the foul cesspit of the metropolis."

"I was not referring to the moral character of the inhabitants," I told him, with a laugh.

"And speaking of inhabitants – ah!" he exclaimed, as the door opened, to reveal the heavy form and distinctive black beard of the famous Professor Harrington, whom I recognised from the photographs that appeared from time to time in the illustrated magazines.

"Holmes, my man!" he fairly bellowed. "Delighted to see you here. And you, too, Doctor. May I say what a pleasure it always is to read your accounts of the adventures of our mutual friend here. Come, meet the others." He ushered us inside, and introduced us to Dr. Lippenschutz of Leipzig, and Professor King of Oxford. The German was a short slight blond bespectacled creature, albeit with a splendid waxed moustache, while King was of average height and build, and had the appearance of a respectable tradesman rather than a world-renowned scholar. Holmes appeared somewhat surprised to see the German, but he made no comment as the introductions were made.

Harrington, as I have said, was a tall man, as tall as Holmes, though of markedly heavier build. His voice rang out as he made the introductions, explaining that Lippenschutz was Germany's foremost expert on the Anglo-Saxons who had made their way to our shores centuries earlier, and that King had extensive knowledge of the crafts of that time, including metalworking and silversmithing.

"I fail to see," Lippenschutz addressed Harrington in a strong German accent, "why you have invited Sherlock Holmes to join us, Professor. I know of his reputation in the field of criminal activities, of course, but," he added in a tone that dripped with sarcasm, "I am unaware of his achievements in the field of archeology to which I have devoted my life."

"Mr. Holmes," replied Harrington with a little heat, " has been of considerable assistance to me on a number of occasions. No-one doubts your expertise and your knowledge, Herr Doktor, but it seems to me that sometimes we scholars might welcome a breath of fresh air from outside the cloisters, eh, King?"

On being thus appealed to, King, nodded vigorously. "Oh, quite so, quite so," he said in soothing tones.

During this exchange Holmes had been standing by quietly, a half-smile playing about his lips. He now spoke. "Doctor Lippenschutz, believe me, I have no wish to usurp your position. I am here merely as an interested amateur, and I would have no wish to infringe on your preserves in this field." He made a half-bow in the German's direction, which was returned, albeit with an ill grace.

"What has been discovered so far?" I enquired.

"Why, nothing as yet," Harrington boomed out. "We have been engaged in examining and recording the external form of the barrow. The workmen have been carefully digging a trench through the sod towards the opening of the inner stone chamber. All being well, tomorrow should see the unsealing of the chamber, and then we, my friends, will be the first to enter that place where an unknown chieftain takes his eternal rest."

"And we will find, I predict," Lippenschutz added in his heavy accent, "many crosses and other items of a Christian nature, proving my thesis that the Germanic tribes crossed the sea, bringing Christianity and civilisation to the British, who had lapsed into their original savagery following the departure of their Roman masters."

Harrington bristled visibly. "And I predict, Herr Doktor, that we will find no such thing. Rather, we will discover the relics of a pagan belief, and possibly even the evidence that I have sought for so long."

It was clear to me that there was much being left unsaid in

this exchange, but being unfamiliar with the beliefs and opinions of the principals in the case, it seemed to fall to me to pour oil on troubled waters, Holmes standing to one side, a faint half-smile on his thin lips. "Hard work digging in this heavy soil, I would guess," I said.

"That is what we feared," King answered him. "However, the work has proved surprisingly easy. I confess to being a little surprised by the speed with which the excavation has proceeded."

"Nonsense," said Harrington, his disagreement with Lippenschutz seemingly put aside for a while. "These are good workmen. I have used them before on previous occasions, and they know well that if they do their work efficiently, they will be rewarded accordingly. It may be true that the soil is slightly lighter than might be expected, though. However," and he turned to Holmes and myself, "it is now time for me to show you your room. I take it you have no objection to sharing?"

The room proved to be comfortable and spacious, and Harrington left Holmes and me to unpack.

When we were alone, Holmes let out a quiet low whistle. "I could hardly believe my eyes when I saw Lippenschutz just now."

"Why? Is he not one of the foremost authorities on this period of history?"

"He is that, but his views and those of Harrington are in direct opposition to each other. Lippenschutz believes, as you heard, that the invaders were a civilising influence on the British natives. Harrington, on the other hand, sees them as having been savages who pillaged and destroyed the society that they invaded."

I shook my head. "And who is to say who is right?"

"That, my dear Watson, is the question that may well be answered when the barrow is opened tomorrow. It is of a special importance, being larger than any other barrow of that period, and also in a location that would seem to be the crossing point of two major roads. Whoever rests in that tomb was undoubtedly a man of great importance, and what we discover in there may well prove to be the definitive answer to the question that vexes Harrington and Lippenschutz. But come, let us go and see the barrow itself."

The monument proved to be impressive. Standing in the middle of a flat meadow, it was boat-shaped, some fifty yards long by twenty wide, and twenty feet or more in height. In the middle of one of the long sides, we discerned a trench cut into the "boat", with the workmen packing up their tools preparatory for stopping work for the night.

"It is truly a fine sight," I said to King, who was accompanying us.

"It is indeed," he said. "The wonder is that no-one has entered before us."

"How did Harrington know where to dig the trench?" asked Holmes.

King shrugged. "You would have to ask him. However, he has calculated that at sunrise on Midsummer Day, the light would pass along this trench to the entrance to the stone chamber, located at the precise centre of the longer side of the barrow. This is a pattern that he has apparently seen reproduced in other monuments."

"Pardon my curiosity," I said to King, "but where do you stand in the controversy between Harrington and Lippenschutz?"

He laughed gaily. "I will make my judgement based on what we see and discover. To date, I believe that there has not been sufficient evidence to come down definitively on one side or the other. To tell you the truth," and here his voice dropped, so that we had to strain our ears to hear him, "I do not believe that either Harrington or Lippenschutz has any evidence to support his theory. Both seem to me to base their views on mere prejudice."

"Your prudence does you credit, Professor King," Holmes smiled. "You are a man after my own heart." Suddenly, he stopped, and bent to the ground, where he retrieved a small object, which he carefully placed in one of the envelopes he always carried with him. I was burning with curiosity to know what it was that he had discovered, but refrained from comment, guessing that he would reveal all when the time was right.

King had likewise noticed Holmes' action, and addressed him.

"I trust that is not some ancient artefact that you are pocketing, Holmes," he said, a trifle sharply. "You should be aware that modern archaeology is more than the mere collection of interesting trifles."

"Indeed so," replied Sherlock Holmes in a conciliatory tone. "Although a mere amateur in this field, I am well aware of this principle, and would never dream of disturbing the strata which are of such great assistance to professionals such as yourself."

This combination of modesty and flattery appeared to have its desired effect, and King forbore from further comment on the matter. We reached the end of the trench, and King touched the wall at the end, almost affectionately. "Another few feet, and we should be at the entrance, according to Harrington. And then we shall see what we shall see."

"Indeed," replied Holmes. "Pray tell me, do you believe that this could be the burial place of Redwald, the king of this region in Saxon times?"

King's eyes gleamed with anticipatory delight. "We can but hope that this turns out to be the case."

We left the trench and returned to the house, Holmes and King discussing abstruse matters relating to the time when the Saxons held sway over this part of England.

Dinner that evening was a convivial affair, despite the earlier disagreements between Harrington and Lippenschutz. The talk, to my relief, was not solely concerned with the doings of one thousand years ago, but took in many interesting subjects, on all of which Holmes proved himself to be something of an authority.

Not unnaturally, the talk turned to criminal matters, and to some of Holmes' cases.

"I always wondered, Holmes," King remarked, as we sat with the port and cigars, "why you were not employed in the case around here a few years ago."

Before King could amplify, or Holmes could answer, Harrington burst out with, "Ah, King, you are from Oxford, and you may not understand the temperament of the East Anglians as do I, living in Cambridge close by here. The good people round here are suspicious of outsiders, and would not welcome external interference, as they would perceive it, in their local affairs."

Holmes, whose expression during this outburst had been one of quiet amusement, nodded. "Quite so," he confirmed. "It was felt by the local constabulary that there was no need for an outsider to come in."

"But does not Scotland Yard have the power to direct investigations?" asked Lippenschutz. "Forgive the question, but I know relatively little of the police procedures in this country. In Germany, naturally, we do things in a different way."

"Scotland Yard, for all its international reputation, is merely the headquarters of the London Metropolitan Police," explained Holmes. "This area falls under the jurisdiction of the Suffolk Constabulary, who are free to call on assistance from the capital, but are under no obligation to do so."

"And quite right, too," added Harrington. "It would be a confounded nuisance to have the London bobbies tramping up and down, treating our country lanes as though they were the back alleys of the stinking slums of London."

"Your family is from around these parts?" I asked him. There appeared to have been something territorial in his latest speech.

"Indeed so. I was born not five miles from this very spot. The house in which we are now staying was bought by my father when I was a boy, and it passed into my possession when he died, together with a respectable amount of land. Indeed, the meadow in which the barrow stands is my property. In the past, it has been let out to a farmer for the purpose of grazing sheep, but it has lain idle for the past two or three years, as the farmer told me that he no longer had need of it. I return here from Cambridge as often as I can in the vacations, and take a keen interest in the local community, which has resulted in my being made a Justice of the Peace here."

"Indeed?" said Holmes, bowing slightly.

The talk then turned to the duties and the responsibilities of a Justice of the Peace, a title which Harrington bore with apparent pride. When the discussion reached an apparent end, King spoke up.

"If, as we expect, tomorrow will see the unsealing of the barrow, we will have a long day ahead of us. I suggest that we turn in for the night."

I offered no objection to this, and I made my way to the room I was sharing with Holmes, my friend following.

While I was removing my collar, I asked him what it was that he had picked up in the trench by the barrow.

By way of answer, he produced the envelope, and shook out a button, seemingly from a jacket, being too large for a shirt button, and coated with dirt and grime from the trench. "Hardly a Saxon relic," he commented, smiling, before returning it to the envelope.

"I fail to see the significance of that button," I said, "or why you have decided to keep it, let alone pick it up in the first place."

"I confess that there are some points that remain unanswered as yet," he replied. "However, I expect them to be cleared up when we enter the barrow."

We continued our preparations for the night, and I was just about to get into my bed, when another thought came to me.

"Holmes?" I enquired. "Can you remember the details of the case in this village? The one to which you were not invited to lend your assistance."

"Yes, that was a strange case." Sherlock Holmes was already in his bed, eyes closed, but had obviously yet to fall asleep. He continued to answer me without troubling to open his eyes. "As you know, I was not involved with the case, so I can only tell you little more than what is already common knowledge. Two young girls, aged five and seven, the daughters of a local farmer, went missing. The nearby woods were beaten, and the streams and rivers for miles round were dragged, but there was no sign of the children. The general opinion was either that they had been abducted by gypsies, who had been camping in the neighbourhood at the time of their disappearance, or that they had fallen into the mill-race and been swept out to sea."

"A sad case," I commented.

"Indeed so. But as I have said before, these quiet seemingly peaceful villages often conceal more crime than the stinking slums of London, to use Harrington's colourful phrase. And now," he concluded, "I bid you a very good night."

Both Sherlock Holmes and I shared the same ability, in Holmes' case as a result of his unique nature, and in mine hard-won through my experiences in the wilder corners of the world, to fall asleep at a moment's notice. When I awoke, the sun was shining in through the window, and the bed next to mine was empty. I had shaved and was nearly dressed, when Holmes entered the room, flourishing his ashplant.

"I trust we will be provided with a good breakfast," he remarked, drawing off his gloves and washing his hands. "It has been a busy morning so far."

"Where have you been?"

"Over the hills and far away," he replied gaily. "Asking a few questions, gathering information."

"About the missing girls?" I enquired.

He said nothing in reply, but nodded silently. "Mum's the word, Watson," he admonished me. "For the present, at any rate."

We went down to breakfast, which fulfilled Holmes' hopes. "The mushrooms," remarked Harrington with a touch of pride, "were picked by Cook this morning from the meadow by the barrow. They are probably the freshest such that you will ever taste. The pig from which the bacon was taken was raised in the farm next to here, as are the hens which laid these eggs. Good wholesome country food, gentlemen, such as you will not find in even the finest houses in the city."

The meal was indeed delicious, but I noticed Holmes examining the contents of his plate with a sceptical air. I was about to remark on this, when he caught my eye, and raised his finger to his lips, unobserved by the others at the table.

"And now," announced Harrington, when we had finished eating, "it is time for us to enter the Holy of Holies, should all go well."

We took our hats and sticks and followed him across the meadow to the barrow, where workmen were already at work in the trench. Along the way, I noticed many mushrooms growing, similar to the ones we had just enjoyed at breakfast.

We had only been standing for less than half an hour, when one of the workmen cried out to Harrington, "There's a door here, sir!"

Sure enough, an ancient oaken door was now revealed, whose wood had apparently been preserved by the peat-like soil. "Excellent!" exclaimed Harrington. "Come on, men, clear it, so we can have it open. There will be an extra half-crown for each of you if you can do it in twenty minutes."

They fell to with a will, and to my astonishment, I saw Holmes strip off his jacket, seize a shovel and mingle with the workmen, digging and straining alongside them. Accordingly it was much less than twenty minutes later that Harrington, with an air of ceremony, took hold of the wooden latch let into the door, and pushed. "We are the first, gentlemen, to breathe the air in here since the Saxons, over one thousand years before us."

As the door opened, I caught a whiff of the air escaping

from the chamber. Rather than the old musty smell I was expecting, a sharp odour escaped, that caught at the back of my throat. I noticed the others coughing, as we entered, lanterns held high.

"Halloa! What are these?" cried King, starting back. I followed his gaze, and beheld two small human bodies, seemingly desiccated and mummified. Harrington stepped back with a cry of horror, and Lippenschutz seemed about to faint, as he hurriedly stumbled out of the chamber, a handkerchief clapped to his mouth.

"Well, Holmes, you are the specialist in dead bodies, are you not?" enquired King. His tone was faintly mocking. "You too, Doctor, I dare say. What can you tell us about these?"

Holmes and I drew closer to the bodies, and the choking smell became stronger as we approached.

"Female," I said, after a cursory examination of the naked corpses. "Age, based on their size, I would estimate at seven and nine years old, taking into account the fact that the Saxon peoples are generally considered to have been shorter than today's population."

"Perhaps," said Holmes. "And then again, perhaps not." There appeared to be a meaning in his words which nonetheless escaped me, though a horrible echo resonated in my mind.

"But the barrow was surely not built for these two little girls?" I asked, as my inward suspicions continued to grow.

"Almost certainly not," he replied.

"Look!" boomed out Harrington in his enormous voice. He brandished his lantern aloft, disclosing a large wooden boat, looming out of the darkness. We left the poor little bodies, and moved towards the boat, where we saw a skeleton, to which some fragments of golden ornaments still clung, and surrounded by jewels and golden treasure such as I had never seen before, and have never seen since. "Truly, this was the resting place of a high monarch!"

"Indeed so," replied King, obviously in awe of the glittering trove of objects that fell before his gaze.

"But what of these two?" I enquired, gesturing towards the pathetic small corpses. "Why are they here?"

"It is obvious," Harrington replied shortly. "They were sacrificed to accompany their lord and master in that pagan afterlife which the Saxon savages believed they would inhabit. Clearly this man was a pagan. I will eat my hat – nay, I will resign my Chair at the University, should we discover any evidence in here that this man was a Christian."

"I believe your hat and your Chair will be safe enough," said Holmes, but his words were uttered in a tone of voice that caused Harrington to look strangely at him.

"Thank you, Mr. Holmes," he replied at length. "Would that others shared your confidence in my beliefs."

Lippenschutz had by now seemingly recovered, and re-entered the chamber as Harrington spoke. "I grant you," he said, in a voice that still had to recover its full strength, "that this particular burial may not have been a Christian one. But that, sir, should not lead us to the conclusion that all such burials were pagan." He started to cough. "Do you not find, sir," he turned to Holmes, "the atmosphere in here to be somewhat unpleasant?"

King had likewise begun coughing. "I agree with you, sir," he said to Lippenschutz. "I propose that we exit the chamber, leave the door open, and allow the air to clear."

"But the gold? The treasure in here? We cannot leave it unguarded," protested Harrington. "As trustworthy as these workmen may be, can we be sure of them in this matter?"

"Indeed you cannot leave the place without a watchman," agreed Holmes. "But never fear, Watson and I will stand guard, all day if need be, if you can arrange for our meals to be brought out to us here. I take it that you gentlemen are all sufficiently assured of our honesty?"

There was a chorus of assent to the last question, and accordingly the three scholars left, Harrington having first dismissed the workmen, telling them that their services would not be required until the following day.

Holmes and I remained, and settled ourselves on the turf at the entrance to the barrow. Holmes retrieved his pipe from his pocket, and filled it. "There are several interesting aspects to this case," he remarked, tamping the tobacco and lighting it.

"We have a case here, then? I was unaware that anything untoward had occurred."

"My dear Watson," he said. "You have just seen the evidence of two callous and cold-blooded murders. You know almost as much as do I of the circumstances, and it should be well within even your powers to deduce the identity of the criminal."

"I confess—" I began, but Holmes stopped me.

"No matter. All will be revealed shortly. I estimate before 10 o'clock this evening." He drew on his pipe. "What do you make of the smell in there?" He gestured towards the entrance to the barrow.

"Quicklime?" I hazarded. "I have experienced it in the past, used in the cholera pits."

"Indeed so, Watson."

"I have no doubt that you will explain your reasoning in the fullness of time, but for now, I confess to being puzzled."

"Remain so, but I will require your assistance later when, as you say, all will be revealed. For the present, we may enjoy the slow pace of the countryside." He reached in his pocket and retrieved a book, dealing, as I could see from the title, with the Anglo-Saxon invasion of the Celtic Britons. I had no such diversion, but occupied my time by examining the plants that grew around us. As well as the mushrooms that dotted the field, there were many other types of fungus, as well as flowers and grass in profusion.

Wearying of this after some time, I re-entered the barrow, and despite my misgivings, made my way to the two small cadavers resting there. Though the corpses were shrivelled and desiccated, it was possible to discern that the little faces bore agonised expressions.

It was strange to me that the corpses of the two little girls should be in such a state, when their lord and master had been reduced to a skeleton. I went over to the boat and gazed at the long-dead nobleman, a feeling of almost superstitious dread stealing over me as I looked at the gem-studded circlet ringing the skull, and the mysteriously-marked necklace that now lay limply across the ribs and sternum of the skeleton. My surgeon's eye noted an arm that had been broken and set clumsily in the past, and a broken clavicle which had not healed at the time of death.

At length, I had had enough of the past, and made my way back into the sunshine, where I discovered Holmes cheerfully gnawing on a chicken leg, a hamper beside him.

"Harrington has done us proud," he said. "A cold chicken and the best part of a ham, together with appropriate dressings and accompaniments. For that matter, it may not be Harrington's doing that has provided us with this excellent Beaune," and he brandished a bottle, "but maybe his cook, with whom I spent some time this morning picking mushrooms from this very meadow."

"So that is what you were up to before breakfast?"

"That, and other things," he replied. "I spent some time with Farmer Green over there," gesturing with the chicken leg, "ascertaining a few facts. It was Green, you should know, whose daughters went missing, and who also had the right to pasture his sheep here, until Harrington suddenly turned him off the land, without providing a reason."

"That is not what Harrington told us last night."

"Indeed it is not. Some chicken?" he invited me.

The food, and the wine, which as Holmes had promised, was excellent, bearing the arms of Harrington's Cambridge college upon the label, produced slumber, and I stretched myself out on the turf and closed my eyes. Holmes remained seated by my side reading.

I was awakened by Holmes shaking my shoulder. "A fine

watchman you make, Watson," he laughed. "It is now five o'clock, and I fancy I see King coming to relieve the watch."

I sat up and sure enough, the figure of King could be seen coming from the house.

"I am to take watch for the next three hours," he told us. "At eight, Lippenschutz will take my place, and at eleven, Harrington will relieve him. I realise it is an imposition, Mr. Holmes, but if you would not object to taking the watch for three hours from two in the morning, and Doctor, you from five until eight, when the workmen are due to arrive and we will all be present?"

"That will suit admirably," said Holmes. "I trust that suitable arrangements have been made to take care of the inner man?"

"Indeed. I will eat on my return. Lippenschutz will have eaten when he relieves me."

"Then all is well," said Holmes. "Come, Watson, let us return the hamper to its rightful place."

Dinner, in the absence of King, was taken a little early to allow Lippenschutz to eat before he took the watch.

"Time for bed," said Holmes, yawning, at the end of the meal. "The fresh air has not only given me an appetite, but it has tired me."

"And me," I said, in response to Holmes' surreptitious kick to my ankle under the table.

"What in the world did you mean by that, Holmes?" I asked when we were upstairs. "I would have welcomed another glass of that excellent port."

"Never mind that," he said, his eyes shining. "We have work to do, and the game is afoot. I was wrong when I said that the hand would be revealed before ten. It will be revealed at some time before eleven, though I cannot give you the precise hour. But there is no time to waste. Change into the darkest clothes that you have. It is important that we not be seen, and though the moon is far from full, there is still enough light for a careless watcher to be discovered."

I buttoned up my dinner jacket to hide the white triangle of shirt, and followed Holmes silently downstairs. We left the house through the back door, and set off following the hedge by the side of the road.

"This will bring us to the barrow from the other side," he said softly. He led us across a field, and sure enough, the barrow lay before us, the trench and entrance seemingly on the far side of the mound. Once or twice Holmes glanced behind him. "To one end of the barrow," he told me in a whisper, and we moved to one end, from where we could observe both long sides easily. Lippenschutz was visible, pacing restlessly up and down in front of the entrance.

Holmes suddenly gripped my arm. "Look!" he exclaimed, nearly soundlessly. A heavy dark shape, which could only be that of Professor Harrington, was making its way up the side of the barrow opposite to that where Lippenschutz was waiting. In its right hand it grasped what seemed to be a heavy stick. We watched in silence as the figure crested the mound, and made its way toward Lippenschutz, the stick raised above its head.

"Now, Watson! Now!" cried Holmes, springing forward. I followed, but we were too slow to prevent the stick from crashing down on the hapless German's head. Lippenschutz sank, moaning, to the ground, seemingly unconscious.

Holmes had grasped Harrington's hand (for it was indeed he) holding the stick, and I seized the other. Our prisoner struggled for an instant, but instantly relaxed as he recognised his captors. He smiled, but it was the smile of a devil, rather than the genial host whose hospitality we had enjoyed.

"I suppose you think you are clever, Mr. Sherlock Holmes? Well, what's done is done, I suppose, and no-one can prove it, so it would be as well to let me go free, do you not think?"

"You are sadly mistaken, Professor. On the contrary, your ignorance has betrayed you."

"My ignorance, sir?" Harrington was indignant. "On the contrary, I would remind you of my position at the

University. Such a seat is not lightly won."

"Your knowledge of the Anglo-Saxon world may be exemplary, but your knowledge of chemistry is sadly lacking. Quicklime, contrary to popular belief, does not dissolve bodies. Rather, it desiccates and preserves them, as we have observed. The results of your abominable crime are there for all to see."

"You—"

"Do not say it."

"You are saying," I asked incredulously as the pieces of the puzzle fell into place in my mind, "that Professor Harrington here is responsible for the murder of these two little girls who went missing?"

"Indeed so."

"But how?"

"Poisoned mushrooms. Those we ate for this morning's breakfast were delicious, but your cook, Harrington, with whom I had the pleasure of conversing this morning, pointed out many others which will cause nausea in an adult, and death in a small child. She knows the difference between those which are edible and those which are poisonous, and so, I am sure, do you. You prepared a dish of these and invited the two little daughters of your tenant to partake. Previously, of course, you had ceased to rent the land to Green, giving no reason for your doing so.

You then took the little bodies and carried them into the barrow, which you had previously opened with the help of the gypsies staying on your land. You sprinkled them with quicklime in the mistaken belief that this would burn the flesh from their bones, and give the appearance of their having been buried together with the Saxon monarch."

"Prove it!"

"Yesterday I picked up a button buried in the soil forming part of the trench."

"Pah! One of the workmen could have dropped it."

Holmes shook his head. "Not so. The button was encrusted

with mould and dirt. Watson here and King observed me retrieve it from the soil. Furthermore, I had occasion to observe all the workmen this morning at close range. None of them was wearing a coat with buttons that in any way resembled the one I found. That button came from the coat of one of the gypsies you employed as labourers to dig the trench and fill it again, before sending them away on their travels."

"To what end did he do all this?" I could not help asking.

"Pride. Damnable pride. Harrington believes that the Saxons were not Christian, and wished to promote the belief that being pagans, they practiced the custom of killing and burying slaves with their masters. By doing this, he would rise in the world's opinion, and crush Lippenschutz here, whose views are entirely contrary to his. This is a crime planned and executed over many years, Watson, and is therefore the more pernicious for that. Naturally, he used his position as Justice of the Peace to direct the police investigations in such a way as to deflect any suspicion away from him.

"It may well be that the Saxon chieftain in there was buried with Christian relics beside him. I am sure that if such there were, Harrington would have removed them at the time he deposited the bodies of the two little girls in the barrow. Is that the case, Professor?"

"Damn you!" cried the latter, and twisted free of our grip. "You will never live to tell the world of this," he threatened, snatching up a spade that had been left by one of the workmen, and raised it in the manner of a weapon.

"Back, Watson," my friend warned me. "He is like a mad beast, and therefore unpredictable and not subject to the rules of reason."

"Wild beast indeed," shrieked Harrington and rushed at us. His foot caught in a hole left by the workmen's digging, and he fell heavily, dashing his head against a large stone protruding from the soil.

"Dead," I told Holmes, after I had examined the unmoving form.

"I confess I am relieved. I am sure of my facts, but proving them in court might have proved a little difficult. Come, let us attend to Lippenschutz, whom I hear stirring."

It transpired that the blow to Lippenschutz' head was not as severe as we had feared, and the poor man was able to walk back with us to the house.

We gave out the story that Harrington had tripped and fallen while coming to relieve Lippenschutz at his watch, and if the story was not generally believed, it was at least accepted by those who had known Harrington. As for the bodies of the two girls, a quiet word to the local coroner ensured that they were quietly removed, and Green was then informed that the bodies of his daughters had been discovered in London. The remains were given a proper Christian burial, and Elizabeth and Harriet Green are now at rest in Little Melford churchyard.

The Little Melford barrow was duly examined in detail by Lippenschutz and King at their leisure, and the British Museum, along with the Pergamon Museum in Berlin, now houses many of the valuable objects discovered there.

"My regret, though," said Sherlock Holmes, as we walked back from the British Museum, where we had been to examine the exhibits when they first went on display, "is that we will never know whether the chieftain buried there was indeed a Christian. However, there was a space in the necklace around the chieftain's neck that could only have been filled by a cross. We must assume, sadly, that Harrington destroyed all the sacred relics he could discover in the barrow. Truly it is said that history is written by the victors, and Harrington won that battle, though he may be said to have lost the war."

# THE ADVENTURE OF THE SMITH-MORTIMER SUCCESSION

HERLOCK HOLMES' CLIENTS formed a representative cross-section of society. On any day, it was equally likely that he would be consulted by a duke or a dustman. The latter, in his opinion, often offered more interesting problems, and he frequently took on such cases at no charge, seeing them as examples of art for its own sake.

Those cases from the upper sections of society, however, were almost entirely ones that brought in the fees that helped to pay for the rent of the rooms in Baker-street, and for the necessities and little luxuries that made up our life. Typically, these cases were of little interest to Holmes, often involving as they did straying husbands, or wives whose interests had wandered outside the marital home. In such cases, Holmes usually refused to take on the work, and referred the applicants to a jobbing detective whose practice was conducted from an area of London south of the river.

Sometimes, however, a case was brought to his attention where the problem was sufficient to gain his interest. Such a one was the Smith-Mortimer succession case, the full details of which have yet to be released to the public, though the court case filled the pages of the newspapers for several days.

A Mr. Anstruther, a solicitor by trade, sent a letter to Holmes requesting an appointment. In it he talked of "a most curious case of succession, which requires the talents of a man such as yourself to disentangle".

"Hardly legal language," remarked Holmes, as he tossed the letter to me for my perusal. "Let us see what this Lemuel Anstruther has to say for himself."

Our client, when he arrived at Baker-street, proved to be a tall thin man of somewhat cadaverous aspect, about sixty years of age, who peered short-sightedly at us from behind thick spectacles. His smile when he greeted Holmes and myself was nonetheless a friendly and open one, and I found myself warming to the man.

"It goes without saying, I take it, that anything I tell you is confidential. That is, until the matter comes to open court, which I have no doubt will be the case."

"You foresee lawsuits? In a case of succession?"

"I am sorry to say that is so, Mr. Holmes. I am acting for one of the parties in the case, and though any court case will inevitably lead to legal fees, many of which will find their way into my pocket, I am reluctant to let matters proceed so far."

"Tell me more," Holmes demanded. "Will you join me and Watson in a cigar? These are of exceptional quality, and are the gift of a minor European royal family to whom I have recently been of assistance."

Anstruther accepted the cigar with thanks, and the room was soon filled with the fragrant blue smoke that can only be produced by the finest Havana leaf.

"I represent a man named Mortimer, who purports to be a scion of the old Kentish family, the Smith-Mortimers. You may remember reading about General Smith-Mortimer, who distinguished himself in the Afghan wars."

"Not only do I remember reading about him, I had the pleasure of meeting him when I served there," I told him. "A most genial gentleman, if I recall correctly, though I fear I remember him chiefly for that large moustache that he wore."

Anstruther laughed. "Yes, indeed, he was a most genial companion. I served as his lawyer for many years, and I have to say that in that time he treated me more as a friend than as a provider of professional services. I shared many a dinner with him, and afterwards we would sit over the port, with our conversation ranging over an extraordinarily wide range of subjects. Those who knew him merely as a bluff simple soldier would have been amazed at the facility with which he could discourse on different matters.

"In any event, he died some months back, leaving behind him a large estate. The house, farmland, and a considerable sum of money in the bank, as well as substantial investments in shares."

"And who inherits?" Holmes asked.

Anstruther spread his hands in a gesture of helplessness. "There is the problem, Mr. Holmes. The will leaves his estate to any descendants of his American half-brother."

"Dear me. No closer relatives in this country? How did this come about?"

"General Smith-Mortimer was childless. His wife had died in childbirth some thirty years ago, with the infant failing to survive, and he was so stricken by grief that he determined never to marry again. He was the only child of his parents, so there are not even nephews or nieces to whom the property might pass."

"But you are representing a scion of the family from America, you told us just now, did you not?"

"Let me be more precise, Mr. Holmes. I am representing a man who claims to be a scion of the family. If he can prove his claim, the estate passes to him."

"And his claim?"

Anstruther sighed. "Mr. Alex Mortimer has recently arrived in this country from America. He claims that his grandfather was the General's half-brother, and as such, he is the closest surviving relative by blood of the General, his father having died a few years previously, and is therefore entitled to the estate."

"An easy matter to prove, surely?"

"Not so, Mr. Holmes. The General's mother died when the General was an infant. His father was subsequently made the military attaché to the United States of America, and, according to my client, married an American lady there. Shortly after the marriage, the North and the South were engaged in conflict, and she left him to be with her family in the South, where she subsequently gave birth to my client. In the turmoil of the war, all official records of the marriage were lost. It is, as you can see, at least within the bounds of possibility that this man is the General's great-nephew."

"He cannot prove his ancestry?"

"He claims that all records were lost in the war."

"And the General never discussed any of this when he was alive? He never knew his half-brother, I take it."

"He was sent away to school here in England and cared for by guardians while his father was in America."

"Then your client has no firm case, I would say."

"Other than this." Our visitor reached in his pocket and produced a fine old watch, which he held out for inspection. "Observe the inscription on the back."

"'To Aldred Smith-Mortimer, from his father, on the occasion of his majority, 23 September 1882'", Holmes read out. "Indeed, that date would seem to fit the story you have been told. And your client...?"

"He tells me that this was passed to him by his father shortly before he died a few years ago, together with the story I have just told you. The General talked about his half-brother to me several times, somewhat in the nature of a family legend, and also mentioned on one occasion that he had been informed that there was a nephew, Aldred, whom he had also never met. As far as I am aware, few other people are cognisant of these facts."

"There would appear to be a goodly number of conveniently deceased witnesses in this case," Holmes remarked, a little sardonically. "However, the watch, where the age of the engraving certainly appears to match the date given, would argue strongly in support of the claim, as you say. The name of your client, you say, is Mortimer?"

"He tells me that at his mother's urging, he has dropped the hyphenation of his name, claiming that the sound is too aristocratic for the democratic United States."

"But can he can prove his descent from this Aldred Smith-Mortimer other than by way of this watch?"

"The papers are on their way here from America, I am told."

"How did he come to hear of you? Or of the death of General Smith-Mortimer, come to that?"

"The General's death was widely reported in the newspapers here. He was by way of being something of a national hero, after all. However, given the American connection, I felt it only prudent to make some sort of announcement in the American press. I therefore placed notices in various major American newspapers, at some considerable expense to myself, I may say, given that probate is unlikely to be settled any time soon. My client is accompanied by his uncle, who claims to have seen the notices, and who contacted me to inform me that he proposed to visit me, with his nephew in order for the will to be settled. I replied, and the two of them arrived in England a week or so ago."

"There is no conflict of interest that you can see in acting as executor of the estate and also on behalf of this Mr. Mortimer?"

"My interest, Mr. Holmes, is to ensure that my late client's estate is transferred to its rightful owner," Anstruther replied, a little stiffly. "I seek no advantage for myself in this other than the standard fees."

"Of course, of course," Holmes murmured. "But I fail to see what my part in all this is to be."

"My client is not the only claimant on the estate. There is a Scotsman who claims to be a distant cousin, and has some papers that appear to substantiate his case. Should my client be unable to prove his claims, the estate will pass to Mr. MacAllister."

"And you would not wish this to happen?"

"Indeed not. I have taken a liking to the American lad."

"He is young, then?" I asked.

"Scarcely more than a boy. I have been told by his uncle that his father, born in 1861, married his mother at a very tender age – in 1877, in fact, and my client was born a mere few months after the marriage." Anstruther coughed in an embarrassed manner. "It is not for me to pass judgement on these matters, however. Mr. Alex Mortimer is therefore a mere seventeen years of age."

"Tell me more about this uncle, if you would."

"A Mr. Silas Weekes, a fine example of the – shall we say

less-refined specimens? – of our American cousins."

"You have obviously met this Mr. Weekes on a number of occasions?"

"I have, sir, and I must confess that I do not fully trust him or his motives. On one occasion he visited me with my client, and I am positive that he was in liquor at the time. I am not Temperance, sir, but there is a time and place for everything, and I consider my chambers to be something other than a tap-room. In addition to this business of the General's will, he claims to be here to purchase items for resale in America, chiefly small knick-knacks, which I would have considered to be not worth his while. However, that is none of my business. My fear is, however, that Weekes will exert a hold over the boy and help himself to a large share of the considerable fortune that may come his way should the estate be settled in his favour."

"I have contacts in the United States," replied Holmes, "and it may be that they will be of assistance in proving the identity and the ancestry of your client, though I must say that at this stage there appears to be remarkably little straw with which to build our bricks. As to your Mr. Weekes, I am unsure as to how I can help you there."

"At present, this Weekes is the legal guardian of the boy, as long as he remains in this country. I would like you to discover reasons, which I am sure will not be difficult to discover, why he should not remain in that position."

"The boy is a minor. Who would then act as his guardian? Yourself?"

"Hardly that, sir. I would make an application for him to be made a ward of court. Once that is done, there will be no appearance of self-interest when I plead his case against that of MacAllister. I confess to a liking for the boy, not least because his features remind me somewhat of my late client and friend, the General. I would be happy to see him outside the influence of the man Weekes."

"Other than a fondness for the bottle, and a somewhat

questionable line of business, are there any other indications that Weekes is engaged in activities that would make him unfit as a guardian?"

"That is for you to discover, I believe."

"Very well, then, I will take the case and work on your behalf. If I have not discovered anything of significance in five days from now – that is, by next Friday – I will throw up the case, and I will charge you only for the expenses involved. If, however, I am on a promising scent, I will let you know, and we will discuss terms more fully. I trust that is satisfactory?"

"Perfectly."

"Then it remains only for you to inform me of the current whereabouts of Mr. Weekes and Alex Mortimer. Your place of business is indicated on the card you gave me earlier."

"I have it here," Anstruther told him, passing over a paper. "You will also see the dates and places of marriages and deaths, according to what I have been told by Mortimer. Weekes has been less than communicative in this regard."

"By Jove, this is hardly a place where one would expect a man of business to be staying," Holmes exclaimed, raising his eyebrows.

"I am not as intimately familiar with the byways of London as are you, Mr. Holmes," our visitor told him, primly. "I take it that this is not a salubrious district?"

"Hardly salubrious, indeed. On the other hand, it has the merit of being inexpensive, and it is doubtless this quality that has recommended it to Weekes."

"Very well, then, sir," said our visitor, rising to take his leave of us. "You will let me know of developments?"

"Naturally," answered Holmes, showing him to the door.

"Well, Watson? What are we to make of all this?" he asked me, after watching Anstruther hail a cab and make his way towards the Park along Baker-street.

"There is little of interest for you in it, I would have thought," I told him.

"There is, however, a great deal of money at stake, if our client is to be believed. And, as flies to a dungheap, so criminals are attracted to such wealth."

"It would seem unfair to condemn the man on the evidence with which we have been presented so far."

"Indeed it would, and I therefore propose to make his acquaintance."

"Surely that will put him on his guard?"

"It would indeed, were I to confront him in my true identity. I think, however, that Mr. Abe Kingstone will make his acquaintance. While Mr. Kingstone is in course of preparation, I would be obliged if you would draft a cable to Leverton of Pinkerton in New York, requesting his assistance in tracing the antecedents of young Mortimer. You have the relevant dates and places to hand." So saying, he disappeared into the bedroom, emerging some time later in a completely different guise.

I have mentioned elsewhere, I think, that the stage lost a fine actor when Sherlock Holmes adopted the profession of detective. From the casual fashion in which he wore the garments, of a decidedly un-English cut, to the poisonous small cigar that protruded from the corner of his mouth, and the lazy drawl that proceeded from it, one would swear that a man from the Americas was standing there.

"I reckon this will do fine, Watson," he said.

"If you can fool Weekes, then I reckon you will do fine," I answered in kind, smiling.

He touched the brim of his hat in farewell, and left.

When Sherlock Holmes returned a few hours later, he was laughing.

"You met Weekes, then?" I asked.

"Oh indeed, I did. Abe Kingstone and Silas Weekes are now 'buddies', as he would have it. The price I have had to pay was one I am unwilling to pay again. The experience of chewing tobacco is a particularly vile and insanitary one, and as for the firewater that he called 'bourbon' – why, the meanest Irish peasant would scorn to add it to a pig's slops. Some brandy and soda if you would, please, Watson."

I brought him the requested refreshment. "I trust that the experience bore fruit?" I enquired.

"Without a doubt. I certainly share Anstruther's doubts as to Weekes' probity. They remain doubts at present. I posed as a fellow American, here to 'fleece' the ignorant British sheep, and let it be known that I assumed he was in this country for the same purpose. I was regaled with a variety of stories, most of which I may discount as falling in the category of what are popularly known as 'tall tales', and many of which I had heard before, featuring protagonists other than Mr. Weekes. Some of the events related were new to me, though, and I have no doubt that the facts related were, at bottom, true, and were the result of actual first-hand experience. They chiefly revolved around the narrator's skill in cheating others in games of chance. Mr. Weekes, far from being a man of business, is a professional gambler. He is financing this little expedition of his through his skills with cards and dice."

"But there is no proof of any wrongdoing as yet?"

"Nothing definite, other than his own words, which he may easily deny."

"And what of his nephew?"

"Ah, there he was somewhat circumspect. Towards the end of our convivial session, his tongue was a little loosened, however, and he let slip that he fully expected to be coming into a fortune, as the result of his sister having made the right choice some time ago."

"That would seem to corroborate what Anstruther believes."

"Indeed it would. I attempted to draw him out on the subject, but to no avail."

"So what comes next?"

"In my guise of a fleecer of English sheep, I persuaded him to give me the names of some of his victims on whom I might practice my wiles. Since he has already received money from them, there is no question of competition in the area, and he was happy enough to oblige a fellow-countryman. I will visit some of them tomorrow in my true identity and attempt to gain some more information."

"By the way, I have drafted the telegram for Pinkerton," I told Holmes, and showed him the paper on which I had written a few words.

"Capital, Watson," he said, and rang the bell for Billy the page, to whom he gave the telegram with instructions that it be sent off as soon as possible. "We cannot expect a speedy reply, I fear, but the sooner we set the wheels on the other side of the Atlantic in motion, the better. Heigh-ho." He yawned and stretched his arms. "Time for bed, I feel."

We were interrupted by Mrs. Hudson's knock at the door. "Mr. Holmes, sir, there's a young gentleman to see you. Shall I tell him to come by tomorrow?"

"Not at all. Show him in by all means."

The door opened to admit a slim youth, whose face had seemingly yet to feel the razor. His voice, when he spoke, was high-pitched and light, though pleasing, and tinged with a not unpleasing American accent. "Mr. Holmes, sir? It is imperative that I see you now. I do hope you will pardon the interruption."

"I am he. Pray, sit down." Holmes examined the young man curiously. "You are American, from one of the Northern states, and you have been in this country for a little time. You are staying at a cheap lodging-house while you are in London, and it is a style of living to which you are not accustomed."

"Why, all this is true, sir. How did you—?"

"And your name is Alex Mortimer, once known as Alex Smith-Mortimer."

Our visitor sank into the chair, obviously thunderstruck. "They told me you were the greatest detective alive, Mr. Holmes, but I never—"

"Tut, man. Watson will enlighten you," Holmes answered him, his eyes twinkling.

"You must help me, Mr. Holmes. You are the only man in

London whom I can trust."

"You cannot trust Mr. Anstruther, your lawyer."

"Oh, but sir, I trust him, it is simply that I do not know how to find him." He broke off and bit his lip. "I have not mentioned him to you, have I? How do you come to know all this about me?"

Holmes laughed. "Let us drink some tea together. It will soothe your nerves." He rang the bell and commanded tea from Mrs. Hudson, who answered the summons. "As to your query, Mr. Anstruther was sitting in the same chair that you now occupy, not a few hours ago."

"Then I do not need to explain my antecedents to you, sir."

"But I would be obliged if you would explain to me how I may be of assistance to you, and how you came by my name."

"Why, sir, as to the first, your name is the only one I know in London, other than that of Doctor Watson here, of course. I had no idea of your place of residence, but simply jumped into a hansom and told them to take me to Sherlock Holmes, and I was delivered here."

Holmes threw back his head and laughed heartily. "Such is fame. Go on, sir."

"Then you will know why I am here in London, and the fact that I am here with my uncle, Mr. Silas Weekes. In truth, he is not my uncle, and though he calls himself my mother's brother, he is in fact an orphan who was taken in by my mother's family as an infant, and raised alongside her. He is, I am thankful to say, no kin of mine." Here the boy gave a little shudder of revulsion.

"Indeed? That is most interesting. Pray continue. Ah, thank you," he interrupted himself as Mrs. Hudson arrived with the tea, and handed a cup to each of us.

Mortimer took his cup, and sat balanced on the edge of his seat as he told his story. "Weekes is a most disagreeable companion. He drinks hard liquor, and chews tobacco constantly. He also makes his living in what I believe to be a dishonest way – through games of chance where he cheats with cards and dice."

"You have proof?"

"Only what I have observed, and what he has told me when he has been in liquor. I fear for myself, though. I feel my future to be in danger."

"In what way?"

"I cannot tell you. I must not say." The lad appeared to be terrified, but would not say more on the subject. "I can tell you, though, that Weekes has not let me out of his sight since we arrived in England. We have met Anstruther, but I have no idea of where we met him. I could not hear the directions he was giving to the driver when we took a cab. Apart from those visits to Anstruther, I have been confined to the lodging-house for the entire time we have been here, even for those times when he has gone out to ply his trade."

"How came you to be here?"

"Earlier today, Weekes was visited by another American, of the same type as he. A gambler and a cheat from his appearance." I smiled to myself at this description of Holmes in disguise. "Though I was not part of the conversation, I could hear what they were discussing as they drank and talked. Weekes drank heavily, and fell asleep after the visitor had left. I took a little money from the dressing-table, and made my way here."

"And you require protection from Weekes? From something that you will not disclose to us?"

"I cannot tell you," he said simply.

"I do not believe I am breaking any confidences when I tell you that Anstruther consulted me, and he has your interests very much at heart. He would like to be able to remove Weekes as your legal guardian, as he is now, and to make you a ward of court, which would render you free from any attempts by Weekes to take your money, should you prove to be the heir to the Smith-Mortimer estate. It would also, though Anstruther is unaware of the danger you have mentioned earlier, forestall Weekes in that area."

Mortimer sat forward in his chair, and clapped his hands

together. "Then that is positively wonderful news," he exclaimed in his high, fluting voice.

"For now, I believe that we may be of assistance. Watson, you have a day-bed at your practice, do you not? Would it be possible for Mr. Mortimer to spend tonight there?"

"Not here?" I asked.

"I feel it would be unwise. Watson, you may care to lend some night attire and so on to Mortimer, at least for tonight, and perhaps ask Mrs. Hudson to prepare some sandwiches or similar for him."

"Very well, then. If you have no objection?" I asked Mortimer. "In that case, let us travel there. It is a matter only of twenty minutes' walk from here."

"You had best take a cab," Holmes advised. "It would be advantageous if you were not seen on the street."

I collected such articles as I determined might be of use to Mortimer during his brief stay at my practice, together with some food prepared by Mrs. Hudson, and we set off. I noticed that our client avoided physical contact with me, and positively shrank from my touch, however much the cab swayed and rattled and threw us against each other. I settled him on the day-bed, and told him that I or Holmes would visit in the morning, and take him to Anstruther where matters could then proceed.

By the time I returned to Baker-street, it was dark, and a light rain was falling. Holmes had just enquired after Mortimer, and I was able to reassure him, when Mrs. Hudson announced that we had a visitor by the name of Mr. Silas Weekes.

"Ah, I have been expecting him," said Holmes. "Show him in, if you would, Mrs. Hudson."

I was unsure of what to expect as regards Weekes' appearance, but I was certainly not expecting the slim dark man, dressed in a somewhat exotic style, with a flamboyant brocade waistcoat and a brightly coloured cravat.

He regarded Holmes curiously for some time before

speaking in a slow drawl. "I am not sure whether you are aware that your name is famous, even on the other side of the Atlantic."

"I believe that I have an international reputation."

"Say, mister, I want you to find my nephew."

"Perhaps you could give me some details."

"I fell asleep some time this afternoon, and when I opened my eyes, the little varmint had vamoosed."

"Perhaps you can give us some description and a name? That is the usual procedure I follow in such cases."

The other flushed slightly at Holmes' words, and proceeded to give a description of Alex Mortimer. "But this is a waste of time!" he cried suddenly. "I will lay money that he is here."

"I may assure you that there is no-one by that name here," Holmes replied quietly, his hands folded behind his head. "If you do not believe me, though I take strong exception to my word being doubted, you are welcome to make a search of the premises to satisfy yourself."

The other appeared to subside a little. "I know he has been here. On the boat coming over from the States, he could talk of little except Sherlock Holmes. Sherlock Holmes, Sherlock Holmes, until I was fair sick of the sound of your name. Begging your pardon," he added as an afterthought.

"I may assure you I have never set eyes on a man or boy of that name, or answering to the description you have just provided. If you wish me to swear an oath on a Bible to that effect, I am happy to do so."

I was slightly taken aback by Holmes' disregard for the truth, but put it down to his concern for his client.

"I guess I'll have to take your word for it, mister. Wouldn't want you swearing no oaths. But you'll look for him, right?"

"For a suitable fee on success," answered Holmes, naming a sum that appeared to take the other by surprise.

He let out an oath which I will not repeat here. "You sure set your price high, mister."

"The price of fame, I believe."

"D__ you! It seems you leave me no choice but to accept."

"You guarantee to pay this money if I can produce Alex Mortimer to you? Naturally, if I fail to do so, you owe me nothing."

"I agree," said the other, though the words appeared to stick in his throat.

"Then let us set it in writing," suggested Holmes, drawing a pen and a sheet of paper towards him and scribbling a few words.

"Very well," growled the other, taking the paper, and signing it as Holmes requested.

"Watson, you are a witness to this," said Holmes. "Kindly sign and date this, attesting that Mr. Weekes here has undertaken this agreement of his own free will, without coercion of any kind."

"When do you expect to have an answer for me?" Weekes asked.

"I would expect that if you call at eleven in the morning, the day after tomorrow, events will be resolved. Good day to you, Mr. Weekes." It was a clear dismissal, and Weekes turned to go, though with a bad grace.

"I will have his money, never fear," chuckled Holmes when he had watched Weekes disappear down the street. "There is no more to be done tonight, other than to let Anstruther know we will be calling on him tomorrow." He scribbled a few words on another sheet of paper, and gave it to Billy, the page, with instructions that it be sent immediately.

The next morning, before breakfast, Holmes requested me to go to my practice, and bring Alex Mortimer to Baker-street to share our breakfast. Accordingly I set off, to discover Mortimer awake and dressed.

"I am glad you are here, Doctor. It may be merely my fancy, but the skeleton you have displayed in the corner of your room appeared to be watching me all night. I could hardly close my eyes for nervousness."

I laughed. "I apologise. It has been a part of the furnishings here for so long that I had completely overlooked its presence. Come, you need never see it again if I know Sherlock Holmes."

On the way to Baker-street, I informed Mortimer of the visit by Weekes, at which he appeared dismayed.

"Sherlock Holmes means to return me to Weekes?" said Mortimer. "How can he do such a thing?"

"If I know Sherlock Holmes, you are perfectly safe. I do not believe that he has any intention of putting you in that man's power."

We reached Baker-street, and entered the room where Sherlock Holmes stood, awaiting our arrival.

"Delighted to see you this morning," he smiled. "I trust you slept well?"

Mortimer was in the midst of his explanation of how he had been frightened by the skeleton, when he broke off suddenly with a shrill shriek. He scrambled to stand on a chair, and with one hand appeared to be clutching his trouser legs, lifting them, and with the other pointing at something on the floor by the door.

"A mouse," I said. "Never fear, I will dispose of it."

"No, I will take care of the problem," Holmes told me. "And while I am doing this, you may wish to assist Miss Mortimer from off the chair."

I looked from Mortimer to Holmes and back again.

"How—?" asked Mortimer, who appeared to be about to burst into tears.

"Allow me to dispose of the mouse first," Holmes replied.

I offered my hand to Mortimer, and now realised that indeed, I was holding the hand of a young lady, clad in male garb, and with her hair cut short in boyish fashion, but a young lady nonetheless. "Here you are, my dear," I said to her, offering her my handkerchief. "I think it would be best for you to sit at the table."

"I apologise for the mouse," Holmes said, re-entering the room, and pouring coffee for each of us. "My dear Alexandra

Mortimer — your name is indeed Alexandra, is it not?" A tearful nod was the only response. "If you wish to impersonate a man, you must learn certain things that mere males do, and females do not, and of course, vice versa. I am afraid that jumping on chairs, shrieking, and pulling up imaginary skirts is something that very few men do when confronted with a mouse. Your way of drinking tea, perched on the edge of your chair, and with your little finger crooked thus," he demonstrated, "as you are doing now with your coffee cup, by the way, likewise marks you as a member of the fair sex. There are many other little points, perhaps too numerous to mention, but those two alone are enough to convict you of the crime of being female." He smiled, entirely without malice, and Miss Mortimer began to smile back. "There, that is better, is it not? But why the deception?"

"It is not of my choosing," she said to us. "Weekes insisted that I dress as a boy. He told me that women were not allowed to inherit in their own right under English law, and that it was necessary for me to pose as my father's son, rather than as his daughter."

"Stuff and nonsense!" I exclaimed. "What a blackguard to tell you such things."

"Furthermore, he told me that if I were to reveal the truth of my sex, I would not be permitted to stay in England."

"That is likewise a fabrication, Miss Mortimer. I take it, by the way, that you are indeed the granddaughter of General Smith-Mortimer's half-brother?"

"Indeed so. My family is very proud of the family associations. Unfortunately, other than the watch, which Weekes presented to Anstruther at one of our meetings, there is little in the way of hard evidence to bolster the claim."

"Anstruther told us that Weekes had requested that some documents be sent from America."

She shook her head. "That was a lie. There are no documents that would prove that I am the child of my father, let alone his son. He was merely buying time."

"But what," I exclaimed, "could have been his motive in all this?"

"I believe I know the answer to that," said Holmes, "and I hope to have confirmation tomorrow from the lips of Weekes himself. For now, let us enjoy the excellent breakfast that Mrs. Hudson has provided for us, and we will then make our way to Anstruther."

"To what end?"

"Why to inform him of this morning's development in the case, and also to start the legal proceedings that will prevent Weekes from acting as Miss Mortimer's guardian."

"Why, thank you, sir," said Miss Mortimer. "Weekes is a true villain, and I hope that you will be able to make him smart as he deserves. As soon as he read of the General's death in the notice that Anstruther had placed in the newspapers, he seemed to have no other object in life but to obtain the money."

Holmes had rung for Mrs. Hudson while she was speaking, and our good landlady now entered. "Mr. Alex Mortimer, who you see sitting here," he addressed Mrs. Hudson, "is, in point of fact Miss Alexandra Mortimer."

I must give Mrs. Hudson credit for her composure. Without turning a hair, she merely made a small curtsey, and said "Pleased to meet you, madam."

"My question is this," Holmes continued. "As you can see, Miss Mortimer is wearing clothes that do not advertise the fact that she is of the fair sex. I would prefer her to be dressed appropriately, but we are in somewhat of a hurry this morning, and I wonder if one of the maids could be persuaded to part with some garments that Miss Mortimer might wear. You can see her size, and I leave you to judge size and style of the garments. Naturally, I am willing to pay handsomely for such."

"I will ask," was her answer, and she left us.

Holmes addressed himself to Miss Mortimer. "I do realise that these will be serving-girls' clothes, and far from being what you would choose for yourself, but we have little enough time, and I wish to present you as a woman, rather than a man, when we explain matters to Anstruther later this morning. I apologise if the clothes that Mrs. Hudson brings are unsuitable, but needs must where the devil drives."

About ten minutes later, Mrs. Hudson arrived, bearing some garments. "That's Mary-Ann's best Sunday, and Susan's shawl. The unmentionables," and her voice sank to a whisper, "are from Susan. I will let you know the price later, Mr. Holmes. May I help you change, my dear?" she suggested to Alex Mortimer.

Her offer was accepted, and I offered the use of my bedroom for the purpose. When Miss Mortimer emerged in the servants' finery, which was, in the event, far from shabby, though hardly in the height of fashion, it was hard to see how she could ever have been taken for a boy, other than on account of her shorn locks, which still retained a masculine aspect.

"Very good," said Holmes, looking her up and down. "I trust you are not too embarrassed to be wearing these?"

"By no means, sir," she said. "You can have no idea how wonderful it is for me to be wearing skirts again after so long."

"Indeed I cannot," smiled Holmes. "Come, let us away. My thanks to you, Mrs. Hudson, and please pass on my thanks to Mary-Ann and Susan. Wait," and he peeled off a Bank of England banknote from the roll in his wallet. "Please distribute this among the girls and yourself."

"This is far too much money, sir."

"Nonsense," said Holmes. "Too little if anything. Come," to Miss Mortimer and me.

When the situation had been explained to Anstruther, he sat back in a state of astonishment, seemingly unable to speak for a few minutes.

"Extraordinary!" he exclaimed, removing his spectacles, and polishing and replacing them before examining Miss Mortimer through them. "I see it now, but I confess I could never have deduced it for myself."

Holmes explained the situation, and described how Weekes

had called, and demanded that Alex Mortimer be found and restored to him.

"I fear you perjured yourself a little there, Holmes, when you said to him that you had not seen Alex Mortimer."

"I did no such thing," Holmes retorted indignantly. "If you will recall my exact words, I told Weekes that I had never seen any man or boy by the name of Alex Mortimer."

"You were certain even then?" I was, as so often, astounded by the depth of Holmes' perception.

"I was. Now, Anstruther, you are the lawyer. Can we ensure that Miss Mortimer is legally protected from the unwelcome attentions of Weekes?"

"It will be done. By the way, Miss Mortimer, as your lawyer, let me assure you that all that Weekes told you about the laws of inheritance is completely false. You have nothing to fear in that regard, and as for the recent impersonation, since it was not at your instigation, and was done at the command of another, the judges in any court of law will dismiss it from their minds. Holmes, I expect to be able to present you with the court order by this evening."

"In the meantime, said Holmes, we must keep Miss Mortimer safe. Watson's and my humble bachelor abode is, I fear, unsuitable for young ladies. Watson's practice is unfortunately tenanted by skeletons. Anstruther, you are a married man?"

"I am."

"Do you think you could prevail on Mrs. Anstruther to take care of Miss Mortimer for the rest of the day, to give her a comfortable bed for the night, and to assist her to find a more suitable wardrobe? Here is money for that latter purpose." He handed over more banknotes.

"Well, I hardly think..." began the solicitor.

"Thank you," said Holmes. "Come, Watson, I have some purchases of my own to make."

The next day saw Holmes and me in the sitting-room, awaiting the arrival of Silas Weekes. Miss Mortimer, most fetchingly arrayed in a new outfit, was waiting in my bedroom, together with Anstruther.

Weekes arrived at the appointed hour.

"Well, Mr. Holmes, what have you to show me? Have you found my nephew?"

"I regret to say, sir, that I have not."

"Hah!"

"But before we proceed further, I would like you to read this." He produced the document that Anstruther had given us the previous evening.

"What the—?" exclaimed Weekes as he read it. His face slowly drained of colour. "I see, sir, that you appear to have won this game. You have discovered her true identity, and I am restrained from making further communication with her. However, you say that you have not found Alex Mortimer, and therefore I owe you nothing, according to our agreement. I therefore bid you a good day"

"Not so," Holmes retorted. "Wait here, if you would. Miss Mortimer, Mr. Anstruther, please."

The two entered, and Weekes stared with horror at the young lady who now stood proudly and confidently before him.

"You see," said Holmes, "Alexandra, that is to say, Alex, Mortimer has been produced for you, as you wanted. You therefore owe me the agreed-upon sum. Mr. Anstruther, as a lawyer, you would agree?"

"Indubitably."

"However," Holmes went on, "I am by way of possessing a sporting disposition. I propose a simple game of chance, played with dice. I have been told that you, sir, are familiar with their use."

The other smiled unpleasantly. "I am that."

"And would you, perchance, happen to have a pair of dice with you?"

"I do."

Then I propose three throws each of two dice, throwing alternately. Should you have the higher total score at the end of the series, I will pay you twice the sum you owe me. Should I be the winner, you will owe me no money. However, I will require you to sign a confession of your crimes, and to leave the country immediately."

"And if I do not?"

"I will set the law on you. And you will find that our English law is a far cry from the rough and ready justice that appears to prevail in many of the United States."

"I see."

"Let us sit at this table," invited Holmes. "Do you sit at this side, facing the window, and I will sit opposite you. You have the dice. We will use this tumbler as a dice cup. I take it that I may have the first roll?" The other nodded.

Holmes took the dice from his opponent, placed them in the glass, and threw them. A two and a one. He gathered up the dice and passed them to Weekes.

"Three," sneered his opponent. "Hardly the best of starts." He shook the dice in the tumbler and threw. A pair of ones.

"My throw, I believe. Three against two." Holmes rolled a pair of sixes. "Your turn, I believe, Mr. Weekes," returning the dice to his opponent.

Another pair of ones, and a foul oath from Weekes.

"We are now fifteen against four. I believe I have won. Should I throw two ones, my score would total seventeen, while you, should you throw the highest score possible, would score sixteen in total. The money, if you please, Weekes."

He held out his hand, and Weekes' hand reached inside his jacket, but instead of producing money, his hand held a small derringer pistol. "I'll see you d__ed first, you cheating ___!" he roared, discharging the pistol. His hand was shaking with rage, and the bullet missed his mark, burying itself instead in the woodwork surrounding the window. I moved behind Weekes and pinioned his arms. He struggled, but was unable to escape.

Holmes raised his ever-present police whistle to his lips,

and blew a shrill blast. In a matter of minutes, two constables appeared, to whom Holmes gave Weekes in charge, the offence being attempted murder. "There will be other charges to lay against him later," he told them. "I will be discussing these later with Inspector Gregson."

"Very good, sir," said one of the constables, and Weekes was led away.

"Thank you, Anstruther. I believe you and Miss Mortimer may now depart," Holmes said. "I expect a wire from Pinkerton soon, which should confirm your claim to the Smith-Mortimer estate, Miss Mortimer. Anstruther, please feel free to call on me for any details that you may require. Should the case ever come to open court, I will be delighted to appear as a witness."

"But why," I asked Holmes when we were alone, "did Weekes insist on that disguise?"

"The answer, I am sure, lay in the peculiar property laws of the state of which he is a native. In that state, when a man marries, the whole of his wife's property is transferred to the man, and the woman has no further claim on it. I believe that were Miss Mortimer to have appeared in her true guise, this would have suggested itself to Anstruther or any Chancery judge as a possible future outcome, and Weekes would have been barred from any further interest in the estate. By turning her into a boy, and by feeding her the lies about the British legal system, he ensured her silence, while deflecting attention away from what, I feel sure, were his ultimate plans."

"A very unpleasant piece of work, then?"

"Indeed. Hardly representative, whatever Anstruther may think, of the open-hearted generous nature of most of our American cousins."

I considered matters a little more. "Holmes," I enquired. "Were those dice loaded?"

"Naturally they were. You remember my calling at Maskelyne's yesterday? Those were my purchases. It was obvious to me that Weekes would attempt to use loaded dice, so I pre-empted him, by using a clear glass tumbler as the dice cup. You will recall that he was facing the window and the light prevented him from observing me closely, even if he suspected foul play. My first throw, he passed to me with a pair of dice loaded to throw ones. I changed them for unloaded dice, but threw only three, as you saw. I replaced them with the low-loaded dice, and Weekes, not suspecting the dice, but no doubt puzzled that I had not thrown a pair of ones, threw them for two and returned them to me. I replaced them with the high-loaded dice and threw a twelve before passing the low-loaded dice back to Weekes. He was hardly expecting one to be more skilled in these devious arts than himself."

"The biter bit?"

"With a vengeance."

The result of this affair, as the world knows, is that Miss Mortimer inherited the Smith-Mortimer fortune following a brief, but highly publicised, hearing in Chancery, and Weekes was sentenced to several years' hard labour for his assault on Holmes, as well as for his attempted deception. Whether it was Miss Mortimer's new wealth, or her undoubted wit and not inconsiderable beauty, once her shorn hair had recovered, within six months she became the Duchess of Shropshire, married to the young Duke who had recently come into the title. Holmes and I were guests at the wedding, as were Mr. and Mrs. Anstruther, and Her Grace was kind enough to spare a few words for those who had helped to bring about the happy state of affairs.

# The Adventure
# of the Boulevard
# Assassin

"AVE YOU ever heard the name of Jacques Huret?" Sherlock Holmes asked me abruptly one morning. I had spent the night in my old room in Baker-street, as was sometimes my habit when I had been attending a case in the West End late at night. It was always a pleasure to be in the company of my old friend, and for his part, he never failed to show me a warm welcome, albeit sometimes in his own inimitable and idiosyncratic fashion. We had just finished breakfast, and Holmes was perusing the morning's post, while I was scanning the newspapers for items of interest.

"The name means nothing to me," I replied.

"Hah. Such is fame, then. I take it the names of Pablo de Sarasate or Henry Irving are familiar to you?"

"Naturally I have heard of the violinist and the actor. They are well-known exponents of their respective arts."

"Then let me inform you that Jacques Huret is likewise an exponent of his art, and is as famous in his circles as are Sarasate and Irving in theirs."

"And yet I have never heard of him. What is this art that he practices?"

"Murder. Or perhaps 'assassination' would be a better term."

"Then it is hardly a cause for astonishment that I have not encountered his name. If he is so well-known in the circles that you frequent, and I do not, why are you speaking of him in the present tense? Why has he not been arrested and executed for his crimes?"

"Because, my dear Watson, the man is deucedly skilled at his foul trade. I know for certain that he is responsible for the deaths of at least ten prominent members of Parisian society, including three Députés, and the French police estimate that he has committed another dozen murders at the very least."

"And he is still at large?"

"In each case, there was insufficient evidence to bring him to trial, let alone to convict him. Huret's speciality is killing in public places, preferably in the middle of a crowd, in such a manner that the death will appear an accident. For that reason, the Sûreté have awarded him the sobriquet of 'The Boulevard Assassin'. Whoever brings this man to justice will be doing the world a favour."

"I take it that the letter you are reading, which arrived in the envelope with the French stamp, invites you to be that man?"

Holmes laughed. "Your powers of perception do you credit, Watson."

"So you are to go to Paris?"

"No, Huret will come to London."

"For what purpose?"

"Huret has but one purpose in life of which I am aware. François le Villard of the French police, with whom, as you know, I am in frequent correspondence, has alerted me to Huret's forthcoming visit to these shores. You may have read that negotiations between a major European power and ourselves on the matter of naval forces in the Mediterranean are reaching a critical phase. The Foreign Minister of the European power will be meeting our Foreign Secretary to discuss the details of any future treaty."

"And Huret will disrupt the negotiations, by murdering one of the principals?"

"So le Villard informs me. Word has come to him of this plot, from sources he chooses to remain hidden from me."

"But why would Huret do such a thing?" I asked, in some perplexity.

"He works for money. Whoever can pay his fees, which are considerably higher than my own, from what I hear, commands his services."

"But this is monstrous! You told me that some of his victims were members of the French Government? Who would pay for them to be murdered?"

Holmes shrugged. "French politics would appear to be played according to different rules to ours," he remarked.

"And in this case?"

"Le Villard is unsure. He has merely received word from an anonymous source that Huret is bound for England, in connection with this visit by the Minister."

"Why has your French friend not made contact with Scotland Yard?"

"He tells me that he has done so, and requested that they provide a guard for the visiting Minister, in addition to using their agents to forestall and capture Huret. However, he writes that he expects no success from that quarter, and he therefore urges me to assist the police."

"Who will take charge of the operation?"

"I do not know. If it is Jones, I fear the worst. He is completely lacking in imagination, as is Lestrade, and imagination is the key to this business. Gregson, or better yet, Hopkins, would be a better selection, but the choice is not mine to make."

"But you will help?"

"Do you doubt it? And I trust that I may call upon my trusted friend for support and assistance in this matter?"

"I am flattered that you consider my services to be of value."

"Do you doubt my word on that also?" he smiled.

Mrs. Hudson entered, bearing a telegram, which she handed to Holmes, who ripped it open and scanned the contents.

"It is Stanley Hopkins," he announced. "Excellent news. He proposes to call here at ten this morning. I trust you will be present, Watson?"

"I believe that will be possible. My practice is none too demanding at present."

Hopkins arrived at the appointed hour, and produced the letter that le Villard had sent to Scotland Yard.

"It's the first that I've heard of this Huret character, Mr. Holmes. Are you familiar with his name?"

Sherlock Holmes proceeded to explain to the astonished policeman what he knew of Jacques Huret and his reputation.

"You are telling me that he murders in broad daylight,

without anyone being the wiser?" he asked.

"Oh, they may suspect that the deaths were not acciden-tal, of course. But to prove that a man did not accidentally fall from the kerb under the hoofs of a carriage-horse, or that the brick that fell from a building roof and crushed a man's skull was deliberately dropped, or that a loose cobblestone caused a man to trip and strike his head against the ground? These are the kind of so-called accidents that befall Huret's victims."

"Then it would seem a simple matter to follow the man wherever he goes, and keep careful watch on him?"

Holmes shook his head gravely. "Le Villard and his men are far from being fools. I hope you will not take it amiss when I tell you that the organisation of the French police is in many ways superior to our own. Huret is a master of disguise and of subtlety. It is believed, for example, that in one instance he entered a café in the guise of a Catholic priest, and left it not three minutes later as a woman of the streets. Furthermore, none of the café patrons recall his even entering, let alone transforming himself."

"How would he accomplish that?" asked Hopkins, curiously.

"A reversible soutane that transformed into a woman's coat was the principal element in this disguise, similar in its basic concept to the overcoat that you have seen me wear on a num-ber of occasions, Watson. The shovel hat worn by the priest was likewise reversible and took on the form of female head-gear, the broad brim concealing the face. A wig carried in the priest's Gladstone bag completed the disguise."

"How did all these details come to light?"

"Huret was kind enough, after he had made his escape, to send the items to the Paris Prefect, together with a descrip-tion of how they had been used. He seems to possess a sense of humour that is all his own."

"So we may safely ignore any priests we encounter?" asked Hopkins. "He is unlikely to use the same disguise twice."

"I would not wager on that," Holmes answered him. "There are elements of bluff and double-bluff. I would strongly advise against you or any of your officers believing that you have an edge over him in the matters of intelligence and cunning. I mean no disrespect," he added hastily. "I would merely state that Huret possesses considerably more than the average amount of both qualities, and it would be dangerous to underestimate him."

"The task of the police," said Hopkins, "would appear to be twofold. In the first instance, we must protect the visiting Minister from harm. I believe, that after our experiences with the Fenian troublemakers that we have encountered, such a task would be well within our capability."

"I warn you, do not underestimate Huret's powers," Holmes repeated.

"You should not underestimate ours," Hopkins retorted, though without apparent anger. "Secondly, there is the task of tracking, identifying, and capturing this Huret. And there, I confess, we are at sea."

"Maybe it would be helpful if Huret's paymaster was identified," I said. "It might be possible to trace him through that route."

"That seems to be an excellent idea," said Hopkins. "Mr. Holmes, what do you think of it?"

"I fear it would be doomed to failure," Holmes answered sadly. "It is almost certain that Huret has been recruited at third or fourth hand, and finding the ultimate source of the funds might well prove a near-impossible task. However, based on the current political situation, we may make an informed guess that one of the Queen's grandsons, who currently is the Emperor of an empire across the sea, is the moving force in this matter. It would be to the advantage of his country's navy were this treaty never to be signed."

"You are out of my league there," said Hopkins. "I cannot begin to understand the complexities you describe."

"Le Villard has requested me to assist you to the best of my ability, as you know, and I will be happy to oblige in this regard. As you are probably aware, Hopkins, my brother Mycroft occupies a position of some importance in the Government, and we should be able to draw on his knowledge of these things should it become necessary. But for now, let us treat the matter as if it were a simple criminal case, with no political overtones."

"I hardly know where to begin," complained the police agent.

"There is one place where you might begin your operations," smiled Holmes, "which would probably be of enormous benefit."

"That being?"

"Watson and myself should be sworn in as special constables for the duration of this case," said Holmes. "Should I discover Huret before you and your men do so, it would be advisable for me to have the full force of the law at my back."

"It shall be done," said Hopkins, making a memorandum in his notebook. "But please ensure that you respect the restrictions imposed, as well as the privileges accorded to that position."

"Naturally."

"And now I shall return to the Yard to draw up the plans for protecting the Minister. I take it you would have no objection to casting your eyes over them once I have completed the draft."

"By all means."

Hopkins left us, and Holmes and I were left alone.

"I share Hopkins' bewilderment," I said to Holmes. "I cannot for the life of me work out where we should begin."

"The places where we should begin," Holmes answered me, "are the places where Huret will expect this adventure to end. Come, Watson, the fog has lifted for once, and it is a fine day to explore London from the viewpoint of a potential assassin."

As we walked, Holmes explained his reasoning. "We can easily expect that Huret will choose a place where there are likely to be crowds. I have already obtained the Minister's itinerary from Mycroft—"

"Already?" I asked.

"Yes. He feared that there might be some popular opposition to the Minister's visit, given the recent troubles in North
Africa, and wished to have my opinion of the various locations that would be in use during the time the Minister is in
England. I was therefore able to recommend that he and his
retinue stay at the Hotel Cosmopolitan, where I know many of
the senior staff personally, and can vouch for the efficiency of
their methods. This is our first port of call."

As Holmes had said, his name and reputation were well-
known in the magnificent hostelry, which had often formed
the London residence of the nobility, and on occasion the roy-
alty, of Europe.

Without mentioning Huret by name, or indeed, providing
too many details, he explained to Herr Vogel, the Swiss manager of the hotel, that the Minister's safety was of great concern to the British government and that he, Holmes, had been
asked to judge the security arrangements.

"We must look, Watson," he said to me, as we began our
examination of the suite which was to be occupied by the
Minister, "for those little things that the police would almost
certainly overlook. We are not dealing with a man who relies
on violence to achieve his ends, but who uses stealth and cunning to work his evil plots. For example," pointing to the short
flight of three steps that led from the suite's sitting-room
down into the bedroom, "what do you think would be the result if I were to loosen the stair-rods?"

"Why, anyone descending would almost certainly fall, and
quite likely strike his head against this pillar," I answered.

"Exactly. And it would be a simple matter, would it not, for
Huret to pose as a hotel servant, and in that guise loosen the
stair-rods when the suite was unoccupied. Following the accident, he might well be called in to assist, and he could then re-
place things as they were."

"He could simply place a tripwire at the top of these steps, and remove it following an accident," I said.

"Bravo, Watson! You are learning to think like an assassin. The ability to slip into your opponent's mind and anticipate his movements is one that is most valuable in this business. It seems to be a trick of the mind that eludes most of our official guardians of the law."

In this way, Holmes and I went through the suite, examining the arrangement of the rooms and the furnishings. By the time we were done, I had filled five pages of my notebook with our observations.

"And that is just the suite where he will stay," I remarked. "We should also examine the public rooms."

"I am going to recommend," said Holmes, "that the Minister does not leave this suite while he is in the hotel. Hopkins may place two constables outside the door at all times, and they will be furnished with a list, including photographs, of all hotel employees who will have occasion to enter the suite. No-one who is not on that list is to be admitted, whether the Minister is in residence or not."

I was filled with admiration by the way in which Holmes had provided a solution which would ensure the Minister's safety and said as much.

He shrugged. "It is true that we have been able to propose a solution in a matter of minutes, where a Government committee would have taken weeks" (I secretly valued the "we" in that statement) "but this is just one of the locations, albeit the one where he will spend most time, where I consider the Minister's life to be in danger. We have much work to do."

Holmes was correct. We spent a long day investigating those places where the Minister was expected to visit, including the Mansion House, where he was due to attend a banquet with the Lord Mayor of London. At the end of it all, I was exhausted, and assented gladly when Holmes proposed dinner at our favourite restaurant in Soho.

"There is one place, however, which we have not yet visited where the Minister will spend some time," said Holmes. "One which I believe you have never visited. And it is one which I strongly advised against, but I was overruled."

"Oh? By brother Mycroft?"

"No, by one much higher than him. A certain widow has expressed a wish to take luncheon with the Minister at her home in Windsor."

"You mean—?"

"Indeed. He will be visiting Windsor Castle."

"But surely he will be safe there? Her Majesty is guarded by the finest soldiers in the realm."

"It is not the time while he is within the Castle walls that concerns me. It is on the road between here and there where I feel that Huret is most likely to make his move. I will recommend a closed carriage and a squadron of cavalry at the very least, but I fear that even that will not be sufficient. But enough of this for tonight. The Lachryma Christi here forms an excellent accompaniment to the sole, do you not agree?"

However, Holmes had, for once, spoken too soon. On arrival back at the rooms in Baker-street, his attention was drawn by a large unstamped envelope lying on the table, addressed in straggling capital letters to "M. Sherlock Holmes".

Holmes rang for Mrs. Hudson, and enquired of her how this message had been delivered.

"I never saw it before, sir, and that's the truth," she answered. "One of the maids or Billy may have put it there. Shall I ask them in the morning? They've all gone to bed now."

"Very good, Mrs. Hudson." Holmes dismissed her, and carefully opened the envelope with the jack-knife from the mantelpiece. "Well, well," he chuckled. "We have a message from our quarry."

"From Huret?" I asked, astounded. "Surely you cannot be serious?"

"Oh, but I am indeed. See for yourself," passing the paper to me.

"Dated today, the 17th. No address. 'My dear Sherlock Holmes, It gives me great pleasure to know that you are involved in the task of attempting to frustrate my operations. It presents me with a little more of a challenge in my work, which I confess to having become a little routine of late. However, I would strongly advise you to cease all such efforts, and confine yourself to the capture of common criminals.' Signed, 'Jean Huret'. Holmes, this is unconscionable. The man is openly mocking you."

"It will only cause me to redouble my efforts to capture him and bring him to justice," said Holmes. "Well, if he wishes to treat this as a game, then I shall play to win." He rubbed his hands together briskly and laughed in that peculiar manner of his which usually foreshadowed the downfall of a member of the criminal classes.

In the morning, Mrs. Hudson brought the news that none of the servants had glimpsed any sign of its delivery.

"I have asked all the girls, and Billy. None of them brought anything up to this room, sir, and none of them remembers seeing anything like the envelope that you showed me last night."

"I see. Very well," said Holmes. "Thank you for your work in finding this out and letting me know."

"So Huret is in London?" I asked Holmes, as Mrs. Hudson made her way down the stairs.

"Possibly, and possibly not," said Holmes. "It may be that a confederate of his, already in London, was responsible for the delivery of this message."

"He works with a gang?" I asked.

"No, no, I am convinced that he trusts no-one. However, there are many here in London who are willing to perform any service, up to and including murder, if a sufficiently large financial inducement is offered to them. In this case, given the seeming importance of the task, I am sure that Huret has money to spend on such a minor matter as having a letter written and delivered." He bent once again to the missive of the day before. "This was not written by a Frenchman – the style of the numbers alone in the date is enough to tell me that." He held the paper up to the light. "And written on English paper, as can be seen by the watermark. No, Watson, we cannot deduce from this that Huret is already in the country, though of course, this is perfectly within the bounds of possibility."

"There is a threat implied in this letter, though," I said to Holmes. "Are you not somewhat concerned that your life might be in danger? You should go armed at all times, in my opinion."

"I will certainly be carrying my riding-crop," he answered me seriously. "It is also possible that you, as my colleague, are in danger. May I advise that you carry your Army revolver at all times."

As you may well imagine, I was somewhat dismayed by these words of Holmes. It is, after all, one thing to face possible death at the hands of Afghan tribesmen in the wild mountains of Asia. It is another to realise that one's life is in danger, walking down a crowded thoroughfare in the heart of the capital of the greatest empire the world has yet seen. Holmes had, of course, experienced such a feeling before, when he entered his final struggle against the Napoleon of crime, Professor James Moriarty, but this was a new sensation to me, and it was far from pleasant.

"I shall certainly do so, if you consider it advisable," I told him, hoping that my voice did not betray my anxiety.

Later that morning, having received notice from Hopkins in the morning post, we set off for Scotland Yard to be sworn in as special constables, as Holmes had requested. In accordance with what we had agreed earlier, both of us were armed, and I confess that I kept looking around me nervously, in a way that I had not done since riding with my regiment through the passes of Afghanistan. Holmes could not help but note my nervousness, and attempted to reassure me. "I very much doubt whether Huret will strike at this stage of the game. He will allow matters to develop a little further before he makes any attempt against us."

When we arrived at Scotland Yard, we discovered Hopkins

in a state of high excitement. "See here, Mr. Holmes!" he exclaimed, waving aloft a sheet of paper. "This was discovered on my desk this morning. None of the porters admits to having placed it there, and no-one knows where it has come from. See here!" He fairly pushed the paper into Holmes' hands.

"Interesting," said Holmes. "It claims that Huret will make his attempt on the Minister's life at the Mansion House banquet. Signed by a self-described well-wisher. Hmm." He handed the paper back to Hopkins, with a look of profound scepticism.

"But do you not see?" cried Hopkins. "This means we may concentrate our efforts on foiling Huret at one point alone. We know the time and the place when he will strike. We cannot help but apprehend him."

Holmes shook his head sadly. "I fear not. The banquet at the Mansion House is the last place he will strike. Consider this." He presented to Hopkins the letter that had arrived the previous evening at Baker-street, and the police agent examined it.

"Why, it is signed by Huret, rather than a well-wisher, but is in the same hand as the letter that I received."

"Well done, Hopkins. And what may we deduce from this?"

"That Huret is the well-wisher who sent the letter to me. Or," he added after a slight pause, "that the letter from Huret was written by the well-wisher."

"Let us assume the latter. It is clear that our man is aware, not only of the fact that we are on the watch for him, but also of who it is – that is to say yourself and me – who will be leading the hunt. I therefore consider it to be unlikely that he will want to spend longer in this country than he has to."

"But how could he have learned of my appointment to this task?" asked Hopkins. "You and Watson are the only ones outside the Yard whom I have informed."

"Then, improbable as it may seem to you, the only possibility is that one of your men is in contact with Huret, either directly, or, as I suspect, through an intermediary."

Hopkins looked crestfallen. "I have no idea what I should do, then, if all my plans are to be given to Huret before they are executed."

"Firstly," Holmes told him, "you must be sure that if you are to make plans, they are communicated to your men only at the last minute." He considered for a short space, lost in silent thought. "Indeed, it may well be a good idea for you to produce false plans and advertise them in advance before revealing the true plans at the last minute. In that way, we may well be able to lure Huret into a trap."

Hopkins looked thoughtful. "When I come to consider the matter, I have not told anyone other than senior officers, about your working on the matter. However, I did write a memorandum to myself, and left it on my desk. I cannot not now locate that paper."

"It is, of course, not without the bounds of possibility that one of your superiors is somehow working for Huret. It may be a matter of financial inducement, or it may be blackmail. Perhaps one of your superiors has a secret mistress hidden away somewhere?" Holmes smiled, and Hopkins returned the smile.

"I hardly think we may suspect Sir Clifford of the latter," he said.

"Perhaps not," said Holmes. "The alternative, and I think this is more likely, is that the memorandum was stolen from your desk. When did you leave it on your desk, and when did you notice it was missing?"

"Why, I composed it two days before I came to see you. I remember distinctly writing 'Must involve Sherlock Holmes and Doctor Watson' on this pad of paper here."

Holmes bent to the pad, peering at it through his lens. "So you did," he observed. "The impression of your pencil is still visible, together with a note to buy flowers for Molly. Your wife?"

Hopkins stammered and blushed. "Indeed, yes, my wife."

"If I may proffer some advice?" Hopkins nodded in response. "I would suggest writing only on a single sheet of paper, and resting that paper on a sheet of glass. In that way, no-one will be able to see the flowers you buy for your wife." Holmes smiled. "But to be serious, who has access to your office? Is it locked when you are not present?"

"I lock it in the evening when I go home or leave the building. If I happen to leave the office, but remain in the building in the middle of the day, it remains unlocked."

"And when did you notice that the paper was missing?"

"Why, the first thing when I returned from seeing you. I came in the office in the morning, having been much exercised overnight regarding the responsibility that had been placed upon me, and unlocked the door. I worked at my desk, and went to Baker-street, after sending you a message that I intended to call upon you."

"And you are certain that you locked the door on that occasion? I mean no slight upon your abilities, but simply would remind you that you had recently been entrusted with a heavy responsibility, and your mind might justifiably have been on other matters."

"As certain as I am sitting here before you, Mr. Holmes."

"Very well. Who else has a key to the office?"

"The Commissioner, the Deputy Commissioner, and two Assistant Commissioners, and my sergeant, Bradwell, whom you may remember."

"Ah yes, Bradwell. Where is he?"

"He has been unwell for the past few days and has not come to work."

"Then he is our man," said Holmes. "Depend on it. He is the man who abstracted your note and left the message on your desk."

"Why do you say that?" asked Hopkins. "He has worked with me for some years, and I am convinced of his honesty."

"All men have their price," said Holmes. "You may consider me an ageing cynic if you please, but the more I see of human nature..." He let his voice tail off, and continued. "Consider. Should you wish to enter a police station, what is the surest way to remain unchallenged?"

"Why, to be dressed as a policeman, of course," I said.

"Say rather, not to be dressed as one, but actually to be one. We may assume that relatively few people were aware that Bradwell was absent from his duties? Indeed, I thought as much. It would be a simple matter for him to enter the building and your office at leisure. Let us see, there is a fanlight above your door, is there not, through which a tall man, if he were to stand on a chair or some such might determine whether you were present or not." He opened the door, and dropped to his knees, examining the floor through his lens. "I thought as much. There are faint indentations here which I think we will find correspond exactly to those left by the chairs here in the corridor on which visitors wait. We may take it that a chair was placed here on at least one occasion. Let us make sure, though, before I visit Bradwell." He examined the lock of the door minutely. "There is no sign of scratching or forcing, such as one might expect if the lock had been picked or forced open other than by a key."

"It certainly does point to Bradwell, does it not?"

"I cannot conceive of any other explanation. If you will have the kindness to swear Watson and myself in as special constables, and furnish me with Bradwell's address, Watson and I will pay him a visit."

"Why you and not I?"

"Watson and I will have the advantage of being police only when necessary. Otherwise, we may be private citizens when more convenient."

"It is highly irregular—" Hopkins began.

"Dash it, man, the whole business is irregular. I doubt if Bradwell can lead us directly to Huret, but he may well set us on the trail."

"Very well then." Hopkins agreed, with a bad grace, and Sherlock Holmes and I were both sworn in as "Specials", with the power to arrest. "He lives in Clerkenwell," Hopkins told us, scribbling an address on a piece of paper and giving it to Holmes. "You will bring him here to me if you learn anything of value. Remember that if you are now members of the police force, you must learn to obey orders, Mr. Holmes." His words were harsh, but there was a smile on his face.

"Hopkins has more sense than to treat me as one of his constables," Holmes told me as we walked out of Scotland Yard.

We made our way to Clerkenwell, and knocked on the door of the house where we had been informed Sergeant Bradwell lived. A woman, presumably his wife, opened the door.

"If you're wanting Jim, he's sick," she told us.

"We had been informed of that," Holmes answered her. "However, our business is most urgent, and it is essential that we see him." As he spoke, he had been slowly pushing his way forward, making it impossible for her to close the door. She shrugged, and offered no further resistance to our entry.

"He's in the back parlour," she told us.

She showed us into the meanly furnished room, where a large burly man in his shirt sleeves was sitting in an armchair, smoking a pipe, with a glass of beer beside him. "Gentlemen to see you, Jim," she told him. "I'm going to the kitchen if you want anything."

"Sick are you, Jim Bradwell? A pipe and a beer is what the doctor ordered, eh?" Holmes' tone was less than friendly.

"Who the ruddy H__ are you to come into my house like this? I'd have you know that I'm a police officer, and I'll—" He broke off suddenly. "Halloa, I know you, don't I? You're that private detective that worked with Inspector Hopkins, aren't you? Sherlock Holmes." His manner changed. "Well, what can I be doing for you, Mr. Holmes?"

"You can tell me who wrote the letters to myself and Hopkins, and to whom you gave the note that you took from Hopkins' desk when you were supposedly sick here at your home," Holmes told him.

Bradwell's face went pale, and he fumbled with his pipe. "Who told you that I had done those things?"

"No-one told me. It was simply a matter of drawing the obvious conclusions from the facts."

Bradwell's voice dropped to a whisper. "For the love of heaven, don't tell my wife about this. Look, Mr. Holmes, I remember you from before. You're a reasonable man of the world. I've— I've made a bit of a fool of myself with the barmaid at the King's Head up the road. Somehow it must have got around, because when I was walking to the station the other day, this foreigner came up to me. 'It would be a shame, Jim Bradwell,' he says to me, 'if your good lady was to hear about you and Edith Clopstone.' Well, that fair shook me up, it did. 'Are you going to tell her?' I says. 'No,' he says back to me, 'if you just do what we tell you.' So he told me to report in sick, but to go into the Yard all the same, and keep an eye open for anything on the Inspector's desk to do with this Huret character. If I saw or heard anything, I was to tell him."

"How were you to meet?"

"If I had anything to communicate, I would place this china dog on the windowsill of the front room." He indicated an ornament on the mantelpiece. If he wished to contact me, I would find a chalk mark on the doorstep, as if left by a tramp. We would then meet at six o'clock that evening in the park."

"Can you say where this man came from? Which country?"

"He was English, as far as I can tell," said Bradwell.

"And who wrote those letters?"

"I assumed he did."

"Were you paid for this, other than with the silence about your affair?"

"I never took any money, if that's what you mean, Mr. Holmes. And that's God's honest truth, I swear it. All I wanted was for my Mary not to hear about my mistake." He looked at us with fearful eyes. "You know what's happened, though the Lord knows how. It's a relief to me that it's out in the open now. But what will happen to me?"

"That is not for me to decide," Holmes said. "We will return to the Yard with you, and Inspector Hopkins can make up his mind. Before we leave, let us place the dog on the window-sill. I want you to meet your friend tonight."

We returned to the Yard with Bradwell, who made a full confession to Hopkins. "It is clear," the inspector told the abashed sergeant, "that you must be punished. However, since Mr. Holmes here tells us that you may be useful to us, we will take this into consideration."

"Now," said Holmes, "we will want you to go to the park and meet your confederate as usual. You will give him a piece of paper, written by Hopkins, which I will dictate to him shortly."

"And then we will arrest your blackmailer," Hopkins said.

"No, no," Holmes corrected him. "We will follow him to his lair, and he will lead us to Huret. The worst possible thing you could do at this stage, Hopkins, would be to arrest him."

"Very well," replied Hopkins, though it was obvious that he did not relish being corrected in front of his subordinate.

Before we set out that evening, Holmes dictated to Hopkins a note in the form of a memorandum, stating that all forces were to be concentrated on the Mansion House on the date of the banquet. "There, that bait should hook our fish," he observed with satisfaction. He persuaded Hopkins, against the latter's judgement, that he and I alone should observe Bradwell and his confederate. "I mean no offence to you, Hopkins," he consoled the police detective, "but I fancy I have had somewhat more experience in these secretive methods than have you."

Accordingly Holmes and I concealed ourselves in a location where we could observe Bradwell. At six o'clock precisely, he was joined by a man in a dark coat, whose most distinctive feature was a large black beard. We observed Bradwell pass the "memorandum" to him before making his way out of the park. Our quarry leisurely stowed the paper inside his coat, before sauntering off in the direction of Farringdon station. We followed him, at a distance, Holmes using all his experience and skill to avoid our being detected by the stranger. We observed him buy a ticket, but by the time we were able to do the same, he had entered the barrier, and stepped onto the train that had just arrived in the station.

"Fool that I am!" exclaimed Holmes. He rushed forward and vaulted the barrier, but the train was already starting to pull out of the station.

Holmes pulled out his authority as a Special Constable, and showed it to the indignant ticket collector. "Quick, man," he demanded of the railway worker. "Did you see where that man was bound?"

"Paddington, I think, sir." This opinion was confirmed by the booking office clerk who had sold the ticket, and who had been watching and listening with some amusement.

"We have no hope of overtaking him," Holmes said bitterly. "Do you have a telephone here?" he asked the clerk.

"Why, yes, sir."

Holmes seized the instrument, and demanded to be put through to Scotland Yard, whereupon he passed on details of the passenger who was travelling to Paddington, and demanded that police officers be stationed to apprehend him, and take him to Hopkins.

"And now we must return there ourselves. I do not hold out much hope of success, but one never knows. Dame Fortune may smile upon us after all."

We returned to Scotland Yard, just as a group of uniformed constables were bringing our erstwhile quarry through the door. "Well done, men," Holmes said to them. "He has given you no trouble? Good. Bring him to Inspector Hopkins' office and keep him outside the door for now."

Once Holmes had informed the police inspector of what had occurred at the park, the man was led in to Hopkins.

"Are you charging me?" were his first words. With his bushy black beard and staring eyes, he was an intimidating sight, but Hopkins appeared to be unimpressed.

"We are well aware that you have been blackmailing an officer of the Metropolitan police," Hopkins began.

"It was a joke, Sergeant," he whined in a small high voice, which was at odds with his physical appearance.

"The rank is Inspector," Hopkins said coldly, and our prisoner shrank back into himself. "And I do not believe it was a joke."

"It may go easier for you," said Holmes, "if you are prepared to tell us something about the man for whom you are working."

"I've never met him," the man said.

"Then how do you get your orders? We know that it is you who wrote the messages that both Inspector Hopkins and I have received."

"Oh, so you are Mr. Sherlock Holmes? I had expected someone a little more... impressive, shall we say?"

Holmes did not reply directly, but fixed his gaze on the other man's shoes, slowly moving his eyes upwards. To those who knew Holmes as I did, it was clear these observations would form the basis for deductions later on. "Perhaps we may have your name?"

"Jack Reid." Holmes smiled at this. "We will take your word for that, Mr. 'Reid'," he said , in a voice that plainly showed his disbelief at the other's statement. "And the answer to my question?"

"We meet every day at pre-arranged times and places. I have never asked his name, and he has not told me. He is a Frenchman, if his accent is anything to go by, and his face is usually muffled by a scarf, so there is little point in your asking me for a description."

"I had guessed as much. When and where is the next meeting?" asked Holmes.

"Tomorrow morning at half past six o'clock. The meeting place for tomorrow is at the entrance to Parsons Green station in Fulham."

"I know the place," Holmes said. "Do not fail to be there. For now, Hopkins, keep this 'Jack Reid' in the cells. We will ensure that he keeps his appointment tomorrow. We may find out his real name at our leisure."

"We have a lead to Huret, then?" said Hopkins, when the prisoner had been removed.

"I believe we have," said Holmes, smiling. "I take it that Bradwell is now safely in custody, by the way? Your men took him in charge on his way from the park?"

"Yes," Hopkins replied. "I have yet to determine what we should do with him, however. If we capture Huret as a result of the information that he gave us, it will be good for his future chances."

Early the next morning, Holmes and I set out for Fulham. As with Bradwell the day before, we followed at a distance. Once more, Holmes had requested that no police officers accompany us, but before our departure, Holmes had quietly ascertained that I had my Army revolver with me. He himself was carrying his favourite riding crop in the pocket of his coat that he had caused to be provided for that specific purpose.

We watched as "Reid" stood in front of the station building, but no-one approached him. After ten minutes of fruitless waiting, he turned, and made his way towards us.

"You seem to be out of luck, Mr. Holmes," he said with a mocking smile. "I believe Huret has not walked into your trap."

"On the contrary," replied Holmes, echoing the smile, "he is here now."

"Where?" I asked, bewildered.

"Why, in front of you. Allow me to introduce M. Jacques Huret," indicating "Reid".

The face of the man in front of us changed to a snarl of fury, and he let out a few words in French which sounded to my inexpert ear like curses, before rushing forward and seizing Holmes, wrapping his arms around him, while whipping the scarf from his own neck. He performed these actions so quickly that before I knew it, Holmes' arms were pinioned to his side, making it impossible for him to move.

"I had planned to make your death appear an accident," spat out Huret, "but you have forced my hand." He wrapped the scarf around Holmes' neck, and started to pull on the ends, with the obvious aim of strangling him, in the manner of the Thugees of India.

"You will never get away with this," I told him.

"I think I will," he laughed. "If the great Sherlock Holmes himself cannot trap me, what is there which allows a mere doctor such as yourself to prevent me from accomplishing my goal and escaping?"

"This," I told him briefly, drawing the revolver from my pocket, and pointing it unwaveringly at his head. He did not release the ends of the scarf with which he was throttling Holmes, but the tension visibly slackened as his face registered his shock. Holmes seized his moment, and using the Oriental *baritsu* skills with which he had bested Professor Moriarty a few years previously, twisted out of the other's grasp and with a dextrous movement flung him to the ground. I rushed forward and prevented him from rising, while Holmes used the handcuffs with which we had been issued as special constables to secure his wrists.

Huret continued cursing in both English and French as we dragged him to his feet, and Holmes invoked the formula of arrest. We summoned a uniformed constable, and with him, led Huret to the nearest police station where we awaited the arrival of Inspector Stanley Hopkins.

"By Jove!" he exclaimed, when the situation was explained to him. "We had the man in custody all the time. Why this charade, Mr. Holmes?"

"Because," said my friend, "we had no definite proof that the man was Huret, or that he was guilty of any crime inside this country. A trial would have been laughable, as he walked free from the dock. As it was, he may be tried for attempted murder, as witnessed by a man of impeccable character, Watson here. And I have no doubt that when the English courts have finished with him, the French judicial system will wish to take its turn."

"I see," said Hopkins slowly.

"Never mind," Holmes told him, clapping him on the back. "All the credit for this stratagem shall be yours."

"But when did you come to the conclusion that we had Huret himself?" I asked.

" It was clear to me as soon as I observed his boots that we were not dealing with an Englishman. The stitching of the sole is of a distinctively French pattern. I am surprised that you did not remark it, Hopkins. And for Huret to involve another Frenchman on this side of the Channel would seem to introduce an unnecessary, possibly weak, link in the chain. Hence I concluded that we were dealing with the boulevard assassin."

"Remarkable," said Hopkins. "I am sure that all of us here at the Yard are more than grateful to you for what you have accomplished."

As we left the police station, Holmes turned to me with an expression of great seriousness and spoke in a soft voice. "Watson, you saved my life just then. Without your assistance, I would certainly have perished at the hands of the assassin. Mere words are inadequate to express my gratitude to you. I cannot tell you all that it means to me to have you by my side as my friend and companion." It was one of those rare occasions when the cold calculating mask of the detective slipped aside, and the human side of Sherlock Holmes emerged. I was touched by his words and the manner in which they were spoken, as who could fail to be, and murmured some inadequate reply.

His gratitude showed itself in a practical form some time later, following the trial and conviction of Jacques Huret for the attempted murder of Sherlock Holmes, the blackmail of Sergeant Bradwell, and conspiracy to murder, to all of which he pleaded guilty.

Holmes, Hopkins and I received a summons from Paris, where we travelled to receive the order of the Légion d'Honneur from the President of the Republic himself. In addition,

Holmes received a personal letter of thanks from Monsieur le Président, together with a not inconsiderable sum of money, which my friend was generous enough to divide equally with me.

# The Adventure of the Two Coptic Patriarchs

HERLOCK HOLMES was a man possessed of many interests, which he pursued in a serial fashion, none seemingly claiming his interest for more than a few months, but at the end of that time, he had acquired such a facility with the subject that he was able to hold his own with world-renowned experts in their field.

I have seen him, for instance, discourse upon Renaissance counterpoint with a professor of the Royal College of Music, quoting from memory, many of Lassus' motets, and their influence upon the liturgical music of Henry Purcell. In a completely different field, his work on coal-tar derivatives, though published pseudonymously, has been described as being the final word on the subject. In the field of crime, and related subjects, he remained the unrivalled master, and to my knowledge there was no-one in this country, or in Europe or America, who came near to possessing his knowledge of the subject, or his skill in drawing conclusions from the facts.

It therefore came as little surprise to me when I visited my friend in the rooms in Baker-Street that we had shared prior to my marriage, and discovered him sprawled on the *chaise longue*, a pile of books and journals relating to the Coptic Church beside him. The air was redolent of some aromatic Oriental tobacco.

"It is an Egyptian blend," he answered my query as to the source of the odour. "I had fancied that it might help put my mind in a mood to understand these liturgical mysteries."

"Why, what are those?" I enquired.

"The Coptic Church of Alexandria," he answered, "is a very old-established branch of Christianity, leaning towards the Eastern Orthodox religion, but differing from it in several subtle respects. To enumerate them all might take the rest of this afternoon, and I will be happy to instruct you in them, if you so desire."

"I think not," I told him. "My life to date has been lived in a satisfactory manner without such knowledge, and I am certain that it can continue in that state for many years to come. But why this sudden interest in the subject?"

He laughed. "I confess that it may seem a little out of the ordinary, but it is a field of interest that was somewhat thrust upon me. A Mr. Mordecai of Golders Green has contacted me. The message arrived this morning, and I lost no time in acquainting myself with the background to the story. See for yourself." He gestured towards the table, where I saw a half-sheet of paper containing some scribbled lines.

I picked it up and read, "'Will call at 2:30 this afternoon regarding the affair of the Coptic Patriarchs. S. Mordecai.' What affair is this? I have seen nothing in the newspapers."

"Nor I," shrugged Holmes. "However, our curiosity should be assuaged in a very short space of time, when Mr. Mordecai makes his call."

It was a matter of only a few minutes before our visitor was admitted. He was a small, wiry man of evident Levantine extraction, with a bushy black beard. His pince-nez had golden frames, and I noted a ring set with what appeared to be a valuable stone on the finger of his right hand. His clothes, however, were not of the most recent fashion, though of good quality.

"Ah, Mr. Holmes," he said, advancing towards me, his hand extended.

"I am John Watson, the colleague of Mr. Sherlock Holmes," I answered him, taking his hand in welcome. "Mr. Holmes is the gentleman there."

"Mr. Holmes," exclaimed our visitor. "It is indeed an honour to meet you. And you, Doctor," turning to me with a slight bow. "Were it not for Doctor Watson's accounts, I dare say that we would never have heard of you, Mr. Holmes."

"I dare say," replied Holmes, with more than a touch of coldness in his voice.

"Not that your exploits would be any the less remarkable, you understand," said Mordecai, having instantly recognised his *faux pas*, and seemingly anxious to repair any damage caused by it. "It is merely that the Doctor here tells your stories in such a way that they cannot fail to entertain those who read them."

"'Entertain'. The very word," Holmes commented drily. "But sit down, sir, and tell us of these Coptic Patriarchs of yours, which have sent me to these volumes."

"Oh, but sir, these are not my Patriarchs. As I am sure you are aware from my name, if nothing else, I am a Jew, and these Coptics are Christians."

"Of course. But you have brought them to my attention, so I may be entitled to regard them as yours, may I not?" Holmes' good humour was seemingly restored.

"As you wish, sir. However, there is the matter of your fee. I am not a poor man, but I dislike spending money unnecessarily." He smiled in self-deprecation.

Holmes returned the smile. "I have been known, as you are aware from reading Watson's 'entertaining' accounts of my cases, as you put it, to remit my fees entirely on occasion. I think I may safely say that, even should this not be the case in this instance, you will suffer no lasting pain when I present my account. But let us return to your Patriarchs."

"Recently I received a package from Alexandria in Egypt, sent by the Coptic Patriarch of that city. It contained a pectoral cross of exquisite workmanship, set with sapphires and other precious stones, the quality of which showed them to be of great antiquity. You may not be aware, Mr. Holmes, that the gems of today, though undoubtedly better cut and set than those of the past, nonetheless are of a quality that is markedly inferior to those of the ancients. The style of the workmanship was unfamiliar to me, though it seemed to me to have elements of the Oriental mixed with the Greek."

"There was a reason for sending this to you? I take it that this item was not being offered for sale to you?"

"By no means. The cross had suffered some slight damage, which nonetheless required a skilled hand to put it right."

"The skilled hand being yours, then?"

Mordecai bowed slightly. "That is so. Or to be more precise, the hand of one of my workmen. The letter accompanying the cross told me that I was to repair the ornament, and that the Patriarch would be arriving in London this month to attend some sort of meeting of churches from different nations. He would call at my place of work to collect the repaired item in person and would make payment for the repair then."

"Ah, the Ecumenical Gathering," I broke in. "A conference of churches from all over the world. I was reading something about this in a magazine only yesterday."

"That is the event," Mordecai confirmed.

"I have some questions for you, Mr. Mordecai," said Holmes. "Firstly, when did you receive the cross?"

"Some six weeks ago."

"And how was it delivered? By post?"

"No, no, sir. Such an item could not be entrusted to the mercies of the postal services. It was delivered by one of the staff of the French Embassy here in London. It had, the messenger explained, been entrusted to one of the French Mission in Alexandria, and transported to London in the diplomatic bag."

"It is a valuable item, then?"

"Mr. Holmes, it would be impossible to put a price on it. Were it to be broken up, the gems extracted, and the gold and silver melted as bullion, I would estimate its material value at a little over twenty thousand pounds. The gems, as I say, are of the finest quality, and there is no jeweller in Europe who would not sell his soul to be allowed to set them. But when the workmanship is also taken into consideration," and here our visitor spread his hands in a gesture of bewilderment, "then it is impossible to set a price on the object."

"And how did the Patriarch of Alexandria come to hear of Mr. Mordecai of London?"

Mordecai smiled modestly. "I may say, Mr. Holmes, that knowledge of the skills of my workmen and my own skills enjoy a reputation that has spread outside the boundaries of this country. My workshop is famous in its own way, just as your work, sir, is famous in your own circles."

"Well, then," said Holmes, "you were given a commission. Was the task an exceptionally difficult one? One which required delicacy?"

"It required skills which would be hard to find outside my workshop."

"And the money offered for your services?"

"Was perfectly adequate. Indeed, slightly more than I would expect."

"And you were to be paid on completion of the task?"

"Half the money, in gold francs, was sent with the cross. I understood that the remainder would be paid by the Patriarch when he came to collect the cross."

"But you have a problem?"

"Indeed I do, Mr. Holmes." Our visitor leaned forward in his chair and spoke urgently. "I do not know who is the real Coptic Patriarch of Alexandria."

"Why? How many can there be?" Holmes laughed.

"Exactly so. That is my question. Yesterday morning, I was visited by the Patriarch. He was dressed in splendid regalia, and I thought to myself that he must have made a striking sight as he strode through the streets of London. He demanded to see the cross, and I was unfortunately unable to present the finished article. Anton, the workman to whom I had entrusted the task, had fallen sick the previous week, and had only returned to work the previous day. I explained this situation to the Patriarch, assuring him that the cross would be fully repaired in two days' time – that is to say, tomorrow. He answered that this would be entirely satisfactory, and left."

"He was alone?"

"He was."

"And the Patriarch spoke English?"

"French. His English was poor, and he was happier speaking French, a language in which I am relatively fluent."

"So all was perfectly satisfactory?"

"Indeed so, until that afternoon, when the second Coptic

Patriarch paid me a visit."

"There are two, then? My reading," and here Holmes indicated the books littering the floor, "informs me that there is only one Coptic Patriarch of Alexandria."

"So I believed until yesterday afternoon."

"This was not the same man who visited you in the morning?"

"Not at all, Mr. Holmes. Quite apart from anything else, this second Coptic Patriarch spoke no French, but spoke very tolerable English. He was at least six inches taller than my visitor of the morning, and of a heavier build. Though both men were dark-skinned, had similar facial characteristics, from what I could discern, and wore the same kind of garment, together with the appropriate regalia, and both had heavy beards, it was still clear to me that I was dealing with two different men."

"This second so-called Patriarch was alone?"

"He arrived with two attendants, who were dressed, I take it, as Coptic priests. I am unfamiliar with the attire of that calling, however. They did not speak – at least to me – but exchanged a few words between themselves in a language which was unknown to me. I repeated my explanation of why the cross was not ready for collection, and rather than the reasonable nature of the morning's visitor, he displayed signs of impatience – almost of anger."

"Surely," I interjected, "in the case of such a valuable object as you have described, do you not take reasonable steps to ascertain the identity of those who will collect it?"

Mordecai laughed. "I am no simpleton, Doctor. Both men produced official documents that seemingly verified their identity. Naturally, I do not have the expertise of Mr. Holmes here," and he bowed once again in Holmes' direction, "but my work involves me in many cases where I need to establish a customer's bona fides, and I flatter myself that I know more than do most about such things."

"I apologise," I told him. "I should have considered more

deeply before speaking."

"No matter," he said. "My question is that I have but one pectoral cross, and two Coptic Patriarchs who will claim it. If I present the cross to the impostor, for surely one of these must be an impostor, my reputation is gone for ever, and with it, my business."

"When will you expect them to return?" asked Holmes.

"The first will appear tomorrow morning at eleven o'clock, and the second at half past one o'clock in the afternoon."

"At your place of business in Golders Green?"

"That is so."

"You have the addresses where these two gentlemen are staying?"

"I do. Needless to say, they differ. Each, however, claims to be staying at an expensive hotel in the centre of London."

"May I suggest that you write to them both and change the venue of the meeting?"

"To where?"

"Why, here, to 221B Baker-street, of course."

"And I will arrange for them to meet each other? Change the time of the appointment to the same for both?"

"Exactly, Mr. Mordecai. You have it precisely. Let us have these two Patriarchs confront each other." Holmes' eyes were smiling as he regarded our visitor. "This promises to be an interesting exercise, does it not?"

"What time is convenient for you?" Mordecai asked Holmes.

"Why shall we not say three in the afternoon?"

"That would be highly satisfactory. With your permission, sir, I will pen the letters here, and submit them for your approval before sending them off."

Holmes indicated the writing-desk in the corner, happily free of the chemical experiments and other impedimenta that so often graced its surface, and Mordecai applied himself to the task of composing the missives.

"Excellent," said Holmes, on reading them. "We now have

our trap ready and baited."

"Shall I bring the cross when I come tomorrow?" asked Mordecai.

Holmes shook his head. "No, let us leave that until we have established the identity of the true Patriarch."

"Tomorrow at three, then?"

"Indeed so."

Mordecai left us, and Holmes turned to me with his familiar quizzical smile.

"And what of this pretty little puzzle, then, eh, Watson?"

"It seems clear enough to me."

"Indeed? Pray explain your conclusion, and how you reached it."

"The first man is the impostor. His lack of knowledge of the English language alone would be enough to disqualify him as the genuine article if he is to attend the Gathering, which will be conducted in English. The fact that he came alone would also seem to argue that his claim is spurious. An important church dignitary would surely be attended at all times by subordinates, would you not agree? But then there is the matter of his reaction to the news that the cross is not ready for collection. An impostor would wish to take the cross as soon as possible, and would become impatient at the news that this would not be possible." I delivered my verdict, based on my understanding of Holmes' methods, with some degree of confidence.

Holmes, however, shook his head. "Your analysis, as far as it goes, makes some sort of sense," he said, "but let me argue the case for the defence. Firstly, both English and French are widely spoken in Egypt. I would consider it quite likely that a man might have a knowledge of one, but not of the other. Second, I do not take it as a given fact that a dignitary must always travel with a retinue. And as for the way in which the news was received, why, it seems to me that Patriarchs may be as prone to the frailties of human nature as any other."

"So you are saying that I am mistaken?" I asked, a little

crestfallen by Holmes' deflation of my deductions.

"No, no, my dear fellow. I am simply reminding you that there may be more than one theory that meets the observed facts."

"And what do you make of them?"

"I prefer not to express any opinion on the matter at present. I am merely going to take the obvious step which Mr. Mordecai, shrewd businessman as he may be, has unaccountably failed to take for himself."

"And that is?"

"I will pay a visit to the Ecumenical Gathering and speak to the Patriarch. Then, when both appear tomorrow, I will know for certain who is genuine, and who not."

I laughed. "You are making it ridiculously simple."

"I see no need to multiply difficulties. And the simplicity of the method and its subsequent lack of expense will, I feel, appeal to Mr. Mordecai's sense of economy."

With that, Sherlock Holmes prepared himself to leave the house, and I, too, took my leave for the day of the rooms at Baker-street where I had shared so many adventures with my friend.

I returned the next day, to discover a client leaving the house, an affair which led to the case I have written elsewhere under the title "The Adventure of the Retired Colourman". As I have explained there, Sherlock Holmes was requested to pay a visit to Lewisham, but having made the arrangements for the two Patriarchs to visit, he was unable to oblige Josiah Amberley, and I made the visit in his stead.

Before I set off for Lewisham, I asked Holmes whether he had been able to meet the Patriarch at the Ecumenical Gathering.

"Ah, thereby hangs a tale, Watson," he said. "To my astonishment, I discovered that the Coptic Patriarch of Alexandria, though invited to attend the Gathering, had sent a message regretting that he would be unable to attend on account of ill-health. This message was delivered through the usual postal system, and through some accident, only arrived yesterday morning, despite having been dispatched a month ago."

"This would seem to mean that both of Mr. Mordecai's visitors are imposters, would it not?"

"It would certainly seem to be the case. The fact of two men adopting the same disguise for the same purpose would seem to me to be more than a mere coincidence, would you not agree?"

"I would indeed. I would dearly love to see them confront each other."

"Never fear, Watson, you will be of more value to me in Lewisham, and I promise you a full report upon your return."

Though this was hardly a satisfactory state of affairs, and indeed was something of a disappointment to me, I nonetheless carried out Holmes' wishes, and the full story of the retired colourman has since been made public. In order to avoid complicating the account of that adventure, which took place concurrently with the case that I am now relating, I concentrated on Josiah Amberley's affairs, though Mr. Mordecai's case was occupying Holmes' energies.

When I returned from Lewisham, and had given my report, I was all agog, as you can imagine, to hear of the meeting of the two self-styled "Patriarchs".

"It never took place," Holmes told me, in answer to my question. "Both men had sent a message to Mordecai informing him that at the time that there was to be a lecture on the Great Schism which they particularly wanted to attend."

"And was there indeed, such a lecture?"

"I sent Billy to the Gathering to confirm this, and the devil of the matter is that there was indeed such a lecture. Whoever is conducting this impersonation is clearly very well aware of the composition of the Gathering. Rather, I should say, those who are conducting these impersonations, for it certainly would appear that neither of these Patriarchs is the genuine article."

"And was either of them present at the lecture? Was Billy

able to ascertain that?"

"Alas, the organisers, though willing to let Billy know that the lecture was taking place, were unable, or, I suspect, unwilling to let him know who was in attendance. But no matter. We are beginning to build up some kind of picture regarding our suspects."

"I cannot see that we have any information worthy of the name," I answered him.

"On the contrary, replied Holmes, without our having even clapped eyes on them, we know something already. First," said Holmes, "it is obvious to me that both men impersonating the Patriarch have sufficient knowledge of the Coptic Church and its hierarchy to be able to imitate the genuine article. The fact that both men wore the same garments and were somewhat similar in appearance would seem to argue that both have the same degree of knowledge. Incidentally, while Mr. Mordecai and I were waiting for our prey, he described their clothing, which corresponds to the description given in the *Britannica*. However, I must also take into account the theory that the criminals, like myself, have access to an encyclopaedia, and I therefore used Burton's account, and some unpublished material from the archives of the Royal Geographical Society, which Billy obtained for me. It would appear that the costumes are correct, as they contain some details that do not appear to be in the published literature."

"So our impostor hails from Egypt?"

"Quite possibly. But let us not jump to conclusions just yet. Secondly, as well as their knowledge of the Coptic Church and its customs, the impostors must know about the cross, and about its delivery to Mordecai."

"That would put them as members of the Patriarch's circle, then."

"By no means. Remember how the cross was delivered."

"By a member of the French Embassy."

"Exactly. Would it not be possible for a Frenchman who has lived in Egypt and was familiar with the Patriarch's appearance, as well as with the customs of the Coptic Church, to get wind of the cross and its repair through contacts at the French Consulate in Alexandria? Indeed, might not the culprit be a member of the Consulate there?"

At this point, we were interrupted by Mrs. Hudson's announcement of "a gentleman to see you, Mr. Holmes, who says it is most urgent", closely followed by Mr. Mordecai, who was carrying a brown paper parcel under one arm, and appeared pale and distraught.

"Mr. Holmes!" he gasped. "I am ruined! Ruined!" He seemed to me to be on the verge of hysteria, and I made a move towards the brandy decanter, the contents of which I have had occasion to use in the past on some of Holmes' more excitable clients.

"Sit down," Holmes told him firmly. "Watson, I agree. A little brandy will do you the world of good, Mr. Mordecai. There," as I passed the glass to him.

The wretched man gulped down the spirits, and immediately seemed to regain much of his composure. "The most terrible thing has happened, sir. See here." He attempted to unwrap the parcel he was carrying, but his hands were shaking so badly that it proved impossible for him to untie the string. I relieved him of his burden, and opened the parcel to reveal an ornate cross, beautifully decorated with gems.

"See here," Mordecai wailed, pointing to the cross. "Look at the gems, Mr. Holmes."

I passed the *objet* to my friend, who examined it closely with the aid of one of his high-powered lenses, concentrating on the sapphires and diamonds that studded its surface. "I see what you mean, Mr. Mordecai, and I understand the reason for your distress. These are clumsy imitations at best, comprised of glass and almost valueless stones. There is no doubt in your mind that the stones were genuine when you originally received the cross?"

"None whatsoever. Believe me, I am experienced enough to know such a thing almost at a glance."

"Your first suspect must be the workman who carried out the repairs – Anton, was it not?"

"He has had no time to carry out such a replacement. Remember that I informed you that he was sick, and has only returned to work in the past few days. It would require more time than this to substitute the gems and to make the repair that he has carried out."

"But he is honest?"

"I have never, in twenty years of employing him, had any cause to doubt his honesty. Indeed, on many occasions I have left the workshop in his care for the evening, trusting him to lock up all the valuable items on which my workmen are engaged, as well as the cash. Never has there been anything untoward in that regard."

"He has no faults?"

"At work, he is a model foreman. However, outside his work, I have heard rumours of a life that might be described by some as being "fast". Women and the Turf, Mr. Holmes."

My friend said nothing, but raised his eyebrows. At length he spoke. "We have a motive, then, Mr. Mordecai. We have the means – he is a highly skilled workman. But he lacks the opportunity if he was, as you say, ill for the period in question."

"There is no-one who had access to the cross while it was with us, I assure you, Mr. Holmes. The cross was kept in the safe."

"Who holds the keys?"

"Why, no-one. It is a combination safe and requires no key to open it. Only I and Anton know the combination, which is also stored in a sealed envelope in my bank, in the event of an accident befalling me or Anton."

"I see." Holmes appeared sunk in thought for a while, and then brightened. "Go home, Mr. Mordecai. I know that it is useless for me to tell you not to worry yourself about this matter, but I think I can trace the gems for you, and discover the identities of the Coptic Patriarchs who have come to plague you. Leave the cross with me – I will gladly give you a receipt for it – and give me two days at the most to solve this little problem on your behalf."

"Now, Watson," he said to me when Mordecai had departed. "Let us pay a call on the Coptic Patriarch."

"Which one?"

"We will first visit the one who is receiving his mail at the Cosmopolitan Hotel – that is to say, the Patriarch who does not speak English."

On arrival at the hotel, we were directed to wait in the lobby of the hotel to await the arrival of the Patriarch. He was indeed an impressive figure, clad in dark robes, with golden ornaments, and a headdress that partly masked his heavily bearded face. It was possible, though, to make out the fact that he appeared not to be of European extraction.

Holmes explained, in his excellent French, that he had come from Mr. Mordecai, and that the cross that he was holding was not yet ready for collection. The self-proclaimed Patriarch appeared to be relatively unconcerned by this news, but merely enquired, in an almost languid manner, when he might expect to receive the cross.

"Why, never," replied Holmes, still using French. "I would advise you, monsieur, to allow me to–" and Holmes leaned forward and tugged at the beard of the supposed churchman. It took very little effort for him to remove it. "A touch more spirit-gum would have come in handy," Holmes remarked pleasantly to the mortified impostor, who sat shivering in his chair as Holmes removed the headdress to reveal a face which, now it could be seen in its entirety, had little of the Oriental or Levantine about it.

Some waiters, attracted by the cry that had been let out as the false beard was removed, had come to our chairs, but Holmes waved them away, demanding that he see the manager. On the latter's arrival, Holmes opened the conversation by asking whether the "Patriarch" had paid his hotel bill.

"Why, no, sir," replied the hotelier. "Naturally, we believed him to be a churchman and therefore allowed him full credit. It would appear, though..." His voice tailed off as he regarded the false beard and the un-Patriarchal face.

"May I leave you to deal with him?" Holmes requested. "I have another urgent appointment. Come, Watson."

"He was not our man?" I asked Holmes as we hailed a cab to take us to the Great Southern Railway Hotel, where the English-speaking "Patriarch" was staying.

"He had no knowledge that the stones had been substituted. Had he that knowledge, he would have demanded the cross, even in an unrestored condition, or at least expressed some more impatience. For the man who has possession of the real gems, it is imperative that the cross is returned as soon as possible in order to avoid any close inspection."

"But when were the stones substituted, and by whom?"

"By the workman Anton, of course. We were told, were we not, that he possessed the combination to the safe, and that he had been entrusted with locking up the business on a number of occasions. From this we may deduce that he holds the keys to the workplace. It would be easy for him to slip from his supposed sickbed in the middle of the night, make his way to Mordecai's shop, and work on the cross in the small hours of the night before returning it to the safe, and locking up the premises before returning to his home and the life of an invalid."

"And the Patriarchs?"

"I believe I know, but we will know more in a few minutes. Here we are." We paid off the cabby, and demanded to see the Patriarch staying at the hotel. As previously, we waited in chairs in the lobby, and were met by the second supposed "Patriarch", who was dressed as our previous acquaintance. He spoke to us in accented, but relatively fluent, English following our introduction.

"You are from Mordecai, yes?" His tones were harsh. "You have the cross?"

"I do," answered Holmes. "I regret to inform you that it is not completely repaired."

"That is of no consequence now," the other told him. "You will do well to return it to me, and I will pay you for any work that has been done."

"I think not," said Holmes. "If you are a sensible man, you will tell me where the stones are, and how you persuaded Anton to work for you."

The change in the other's countenance was almost instant. All the bluster and aggression vanished instantly. His jaw dropped, and he gazed at Holmes dumbfounded. "How do you know it is I who have the stones?"

"We know it is not your one-time colleague, the French diplomatic messenger," smiled Holmes. "You may meet him in prison, I suppose, and exchange notes. Are the stones still in the country? You have not yet sent them to Amsterdam or Beirut?"

"They are upstairs in my room here," the man replied sullenly. "I suppose there is no chance of my freedom in exchange for some of them?"

"None whatsoever," Holmes told him with a set to his jaw that I knew betokened anger at the attempted bribe. "Your name?"

"My name is Safar. Ali Safar."

"I am taking you in charge, Mr. Safar, and will deliver you to the nearest police station, where you may explain how, as a trusted servant in his household, you poisoned the Coptic Patriarch of Alexandria – oh, not fatally, I will give you that, but enough to weaken him sufficiently that he was unable to travel to London. Then you proceeded to purloin the cross, and to ensure its safe delivery to England, into the hands of Mordecai, you used one of the French diplomatic couriers. I assume you paid him for his trouble?" The other nodded. "I thought as much. Once in Mordecai's keeping, Anton would remove the stones and substitute them with glass."

"Exactly so."

"How did you come to know of Anton, by the way?"

"One of my cousins who lives here in London has

connections to the racing fraternity, and met Anton through them. Anton was heavily in debt, and my cousin let me know of the fact that he had access to a skilled workman who could make us all rich. He knew that the Patriarch trusted me with the regalia, and it was the work of a moment for me to damage the cross you hold – not seriously, but enough for it to require skilled repair here in London. As you say, I recruited a French diplomat to carry the cross over to Mordecai, and I left the Patriarch's employ, and took on his identity, having previously informed the Ecumenical Gathering that the Patriarch would attend, and informed Mordecai that I would collect the cross. It was therefore perfectly in order for me to make my appearance at Mordecai's place of work in person. My cousins attended me in order to give substance to the fiction."

"When did you discover that your one-time confederate had also decided to take on the identity of the Patriarch?"

"When I called on Mordecai to collect the cross, it was obvious to me that he was puzzled by my appearance. The conversation revealed that I was not the first Patriarch to have called on him that day. There was no-one except Anton and my cousins who knew of the plan. Anton would obviously have been discovered instantly by Mordecai, and my cousins had been with me all the day."

"So it was Monsieur–?"

"Monsieur Lagrande, of the *corps diplomatique*. I dared not throw off my disguise, but I was reluctant to meet him. I may tell you that one Coptic Patriarch is a strange enough sight in London. Two such would be completely out of the ordinary."

"And when you were invited to Baker-street? Did you know that the Patriarch's letter telling the Gathering that he would not be attending had just arrived in London, by the way?"

The other gasped. "I knew that such a letter had been written, and it was entrusted to me to give to the postal service. I was under the impression I had effectively failed to do so by hiding the letter, but it would seem that I did not do a sufficiently good job there." He smiled ruefully. "As to the invitation to meet in Baker-street, Mr. Holmes, naturally I refused. Your fame is such that 221B Baker-street was an address I was keen to avoid visiting."

"As it was for Lagrande. Well, Mr. Safar, we have chatted long enough, I think. Let us go to the nearest police station. If all the stones are recovered, and they can be reset and the cross returned, I feel that any sentence you receive will be a light one. Of course, there is the matter of your causing the illness of the true Patriarch, but that is a matter for your Egyptian authorities, not our police."

Safar was remarkably quiet and subdued as we went to the police station, where Holmes explained the situation, before handing him over to Inspector Gregson, who had been summoned from Scotland Yard at Holmes' request.

In company with a police sergeant, we visited Safar's room at the hotel, where we were able to retrieve the stones from their hiding place which had been told to us by the prisoner. On our return to the station, Holmes persuaded Gregson to allow the stones to be returned to Mordecai by him.

We made our way to Mordecai's workshop, Holmes carefully carrying the stones in the chamois bag in which they had been hidden by Safar. On our arrival, we were shown into Mordecai's office, where our client was sitting, his head buried in his hands.

"I have the stones," Holmes told him, displaying the chamois bag, and handing it to him.

Rather than being overjoyed, as one might have expected, Mordecai received the bag with a simple word of thanks, and placed it on the table in front of him without opening it.

"Why, whatever is the matter?" I asked. "Are you not even going to verify that the stones are all there?"

"It is Anton," he cried. "Gone! And in such a way, too!"

"What?" exclaimed Holmes. "He has fled?"

"Fled this life. When I returned here earlier today, it was to discover his lifeless body swinging from the beam by the front door. Below the body was a letter addressed to me. Here." He reached in his pocket and withdrew a piece of paper which he handed to Holmes, who read it aloud.

"'To S. Mordecai, I am sorry for what I have done. I know that you have visited Sherlock Holmes and so I know the game is now up. Ask for the Patriarch at the Great Southern Railway Hotel. His real name is Safar, and he will tell you where the stones are. Anton Junger.'"

"What does it all mean?" wailed Mordecai. "I have lost my best workman, and I do not know why. Who is this Safar? And how, in the name of goodness, did you come by the stones?"

"We have just come from Safar, whom we left in the custody of the police," Holmes told him. He added the details that we had discovered.

"My Anton, a traitor? I can hardly believe it," said Mordecai. "I had trained him, almost from childhood, and loved him almost as my own son. I had even intended to hand over the business to him when I retire in a few years. And that he should betray my trust in this way." He spoke not in anger, but with a resigned sadness. "The stones," and here he opened the bag, to disclose a flood of light that sparkled and shone in the sunlight, with all the colours, it seemed, of the rainbow, " all appear to be present. Just one sapphire – ah, here it is. Mr. Holmes, pray examine these and tell me yourself that these are the finest stones you have seen." He passed a jeweller's eyeglass to Holmes, who screwed it into his eye, and proceeded to examine the gems, with cries of admiration.

"I lack your expertise," he said at length, returning the eyeglass, "but I agree with you. The quality of these stones is beyond anything I have ever beheld previously."

"I thank you, Mr. Holmes, for having solved the mystery, and restored the stones, though I wish with all my heart that it had been a happier conclusion to the problem. There is now, I suppose, the matter of your fee."

"In this case," said Holmes, "given your loss that you have

just described, there is no fee." He picked up his hat and stick from the table. "Come, Watson, let us return to Baker-street, where Mr. Josiah Amberley's problem awaits our solution."

# THE AUTHOR

 UGH ASHTON was born in the United Kingdom, and moved to Japan in 1988, where he lived until a return to the UK in 2016.

He is best known for his Sherlock Holmes stories, which have been hailed as some of the most authentic pastiches on the market, and have received favourable reviews from Sherlockians and non-Sherlockians alike.

He currently divides his time between the historic cities of Lichfield, and Kamakura, a little to the south of Yokohama, with his wife, Yoshiko.

More about Hugh Ashton and his books may be found at: http://HughAshtonBooks.com and he may be contacted at: HAshton@mac.com

# OTHER BOOKS BY HUGH ASHTON

*Tales from the Deed Box of John H. Watson M.D.*
*More from the Deed Box of John H. Watson M.D.*
*Secrets from the Deed Box of John H. Watson M.D.*
*The Darlington Substitution*
*The Trepoff Murder*
*The Bradfield Push*
*Notes from the Dispatch-Box of John H. Watson M.D.*
*Further Notes from the Dispatch-Box of John H. Watson M.D.*
*The Reigate Poisoning Case: Concluded*
*The Death of Cardinal Tosca*
*Without my Boswell*
*The Last Notes from the Dispatch-Box of John H. Watson M.D.*
*Some Singular Cases of Mr. Sherlock Holmes*
*The Lichfield Murder*
*The Deed Box of John H. Watson M.D.*
*The Dispatch-box of John H. Watson M.D.*

*Beneath Gray Skies*
*Red Wheels Turning*
*Tales of Old Japanese*
*At the Sharpe End*
*The Untime*
*The Untime Revisited*
*Leo's Luck*
*Balance of Powers*
*Angels Unawares*

*Sherlock Ferret and the Missing Necklace*
*Sherlock Ferret and the Multiplying Masterpieces*
*Sherlock Ferret and the Poisoned Pond*
*Sherlock Ferret and the Phantom Photographer*
*The Adventures of Sherlock Ferret*

7 am 2/14/no

CPSIA information can be obtained
at www.ICGtesting.com
Printed in the USA
LVHW080242280922
729468LV00016B/268